MY SUPER FUN
KINDERGARTEN
ACTIVITY WORKBOOK

THIS BOOK BELONGS TO

....

....

Printed 2023

(An imprint of Prakash Books)

Wonder House Books
Corporate & Editorial Office
113-A, 1st Floor, Ansari Road,
Daryaganj, New Delhi-110002
Tel +91 11 2324 7062-65

ISBN : 978-93-54403-19-4

Printed in India

Fun with Tracing.

Trace the lines and complete the rain.

Start Start Start Start Start Start Start Start Start Start

Sleeping Lines

Trace the sleeping lines.

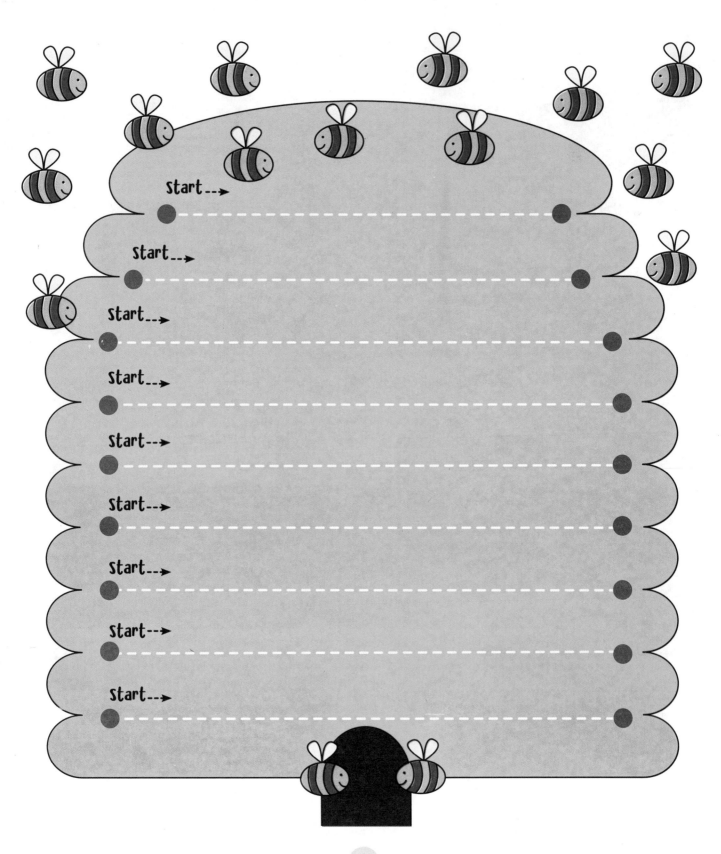

Fun with Tracing.

Trace the lines and help animals reach their homes.

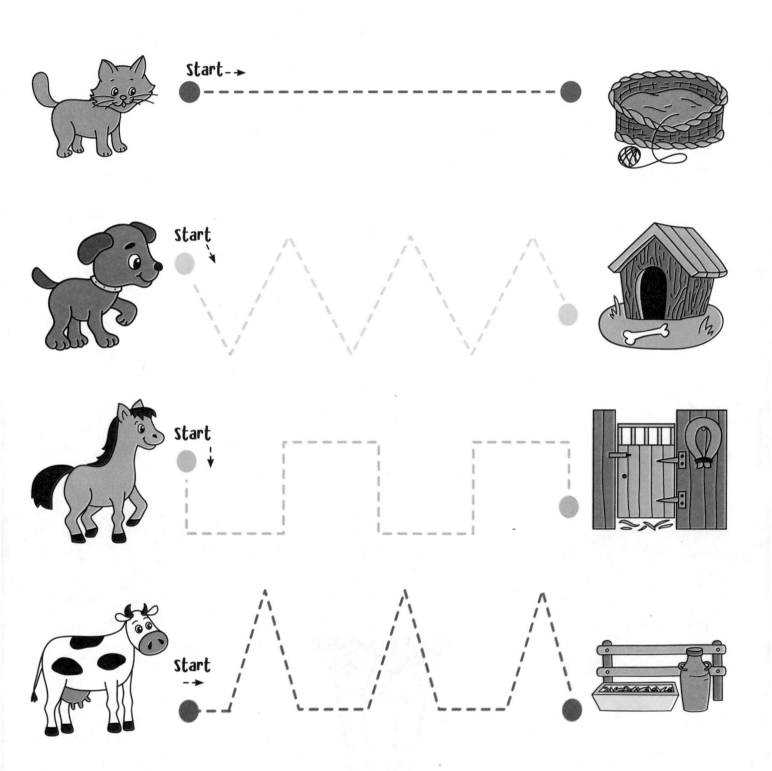

start→

start

start

start→

Fun with Tracing.

Trace the lines and complete the hot-air balloon.

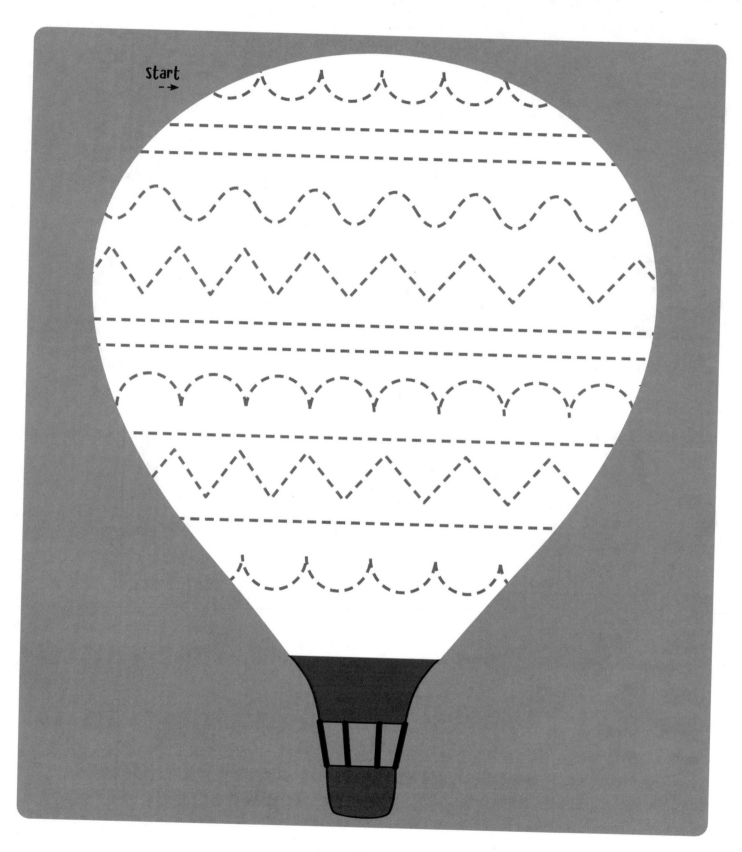

start

Fun with Tracing.

Trace the lines on the crocodile's back.

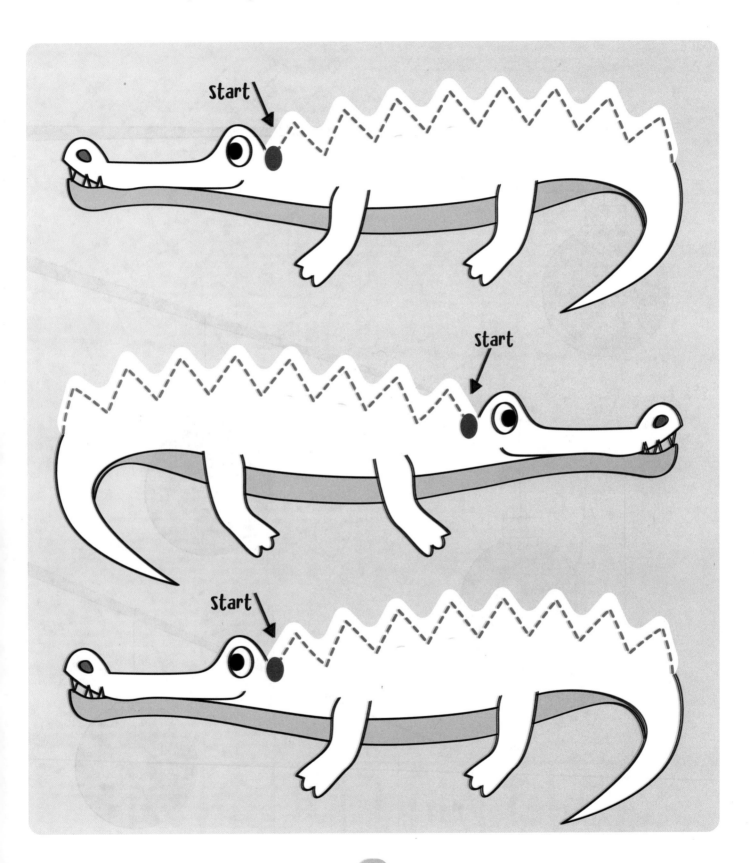

Start

Start

Start

Slanting Line

Trace the lines and complete the pattern.

start

start

start

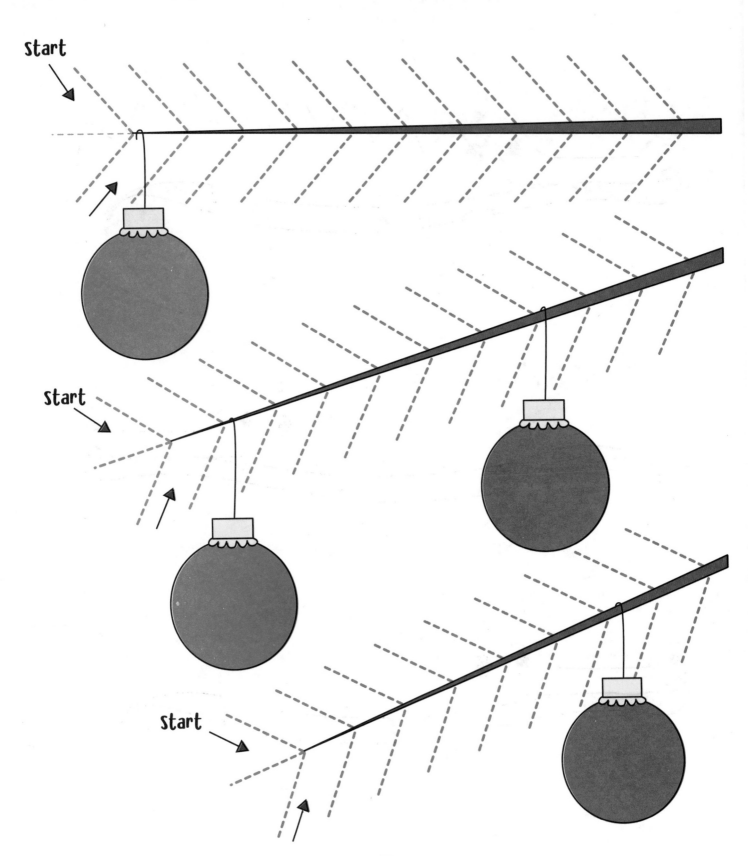

Fun with Tracing.

Trace the lines and complete the pattern.

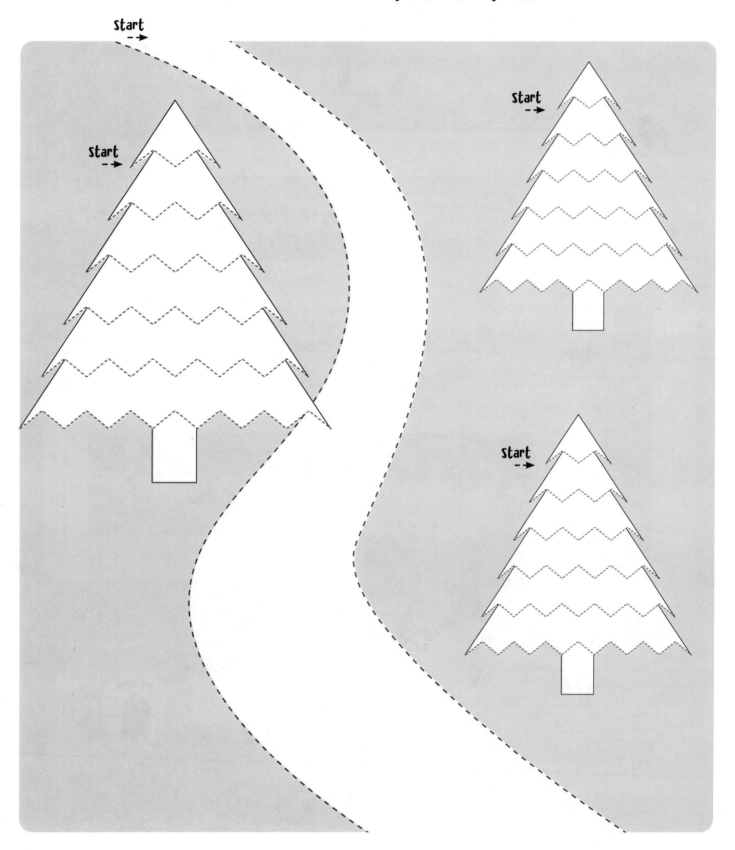

Dog Path

Help the puppy reach its home by tracing the path.

Curved Lines

Trace the lines on the jellyfish's tentacles.

start
→

Slanting Line

Trace the lines and complete the fish pattern.

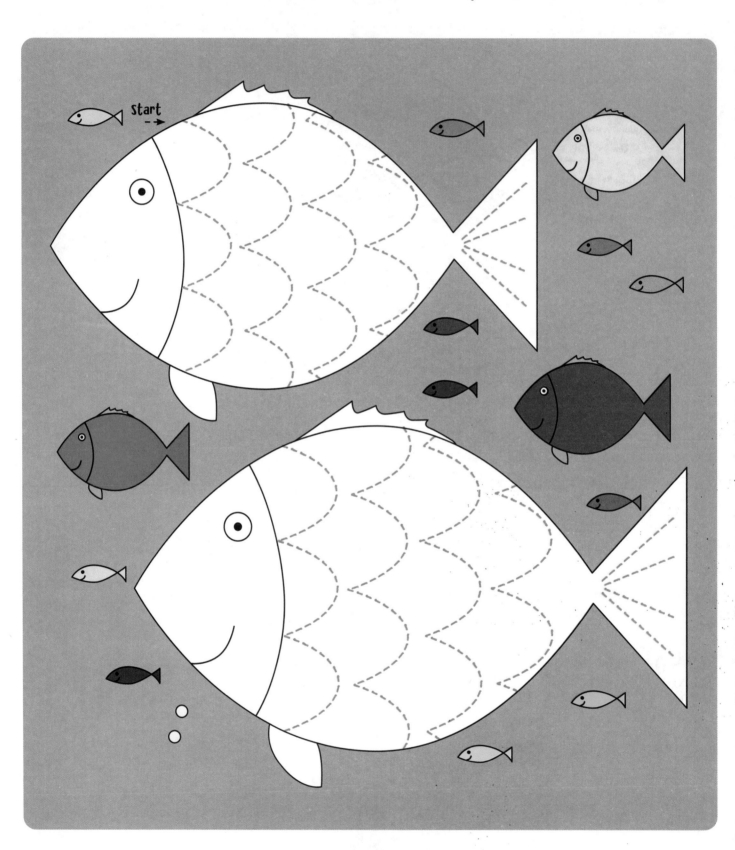

start
→

Fun with Tracing

Trace the lines and help the ships to reach their destinations.

Start

Start

Start

Curved Lines

Trace the lines and complete the sun.

Spiral Lines

Trace the lines and complete the spiral pattern.

Spiral Lines

Trace the lines and complete the snail's back.

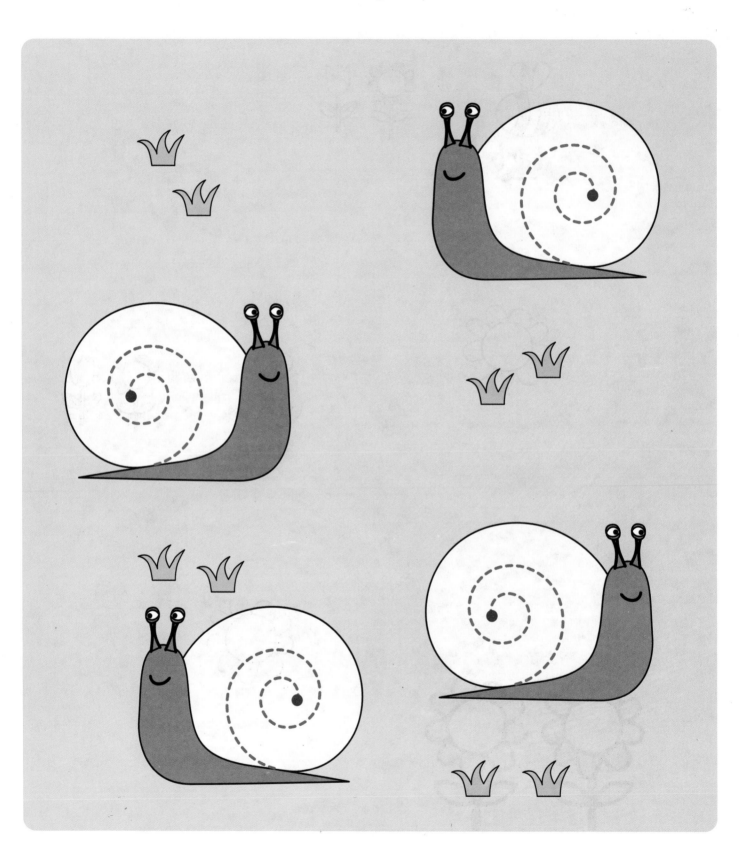

Spiral Lines

Trace the lines and complete the lollipops.

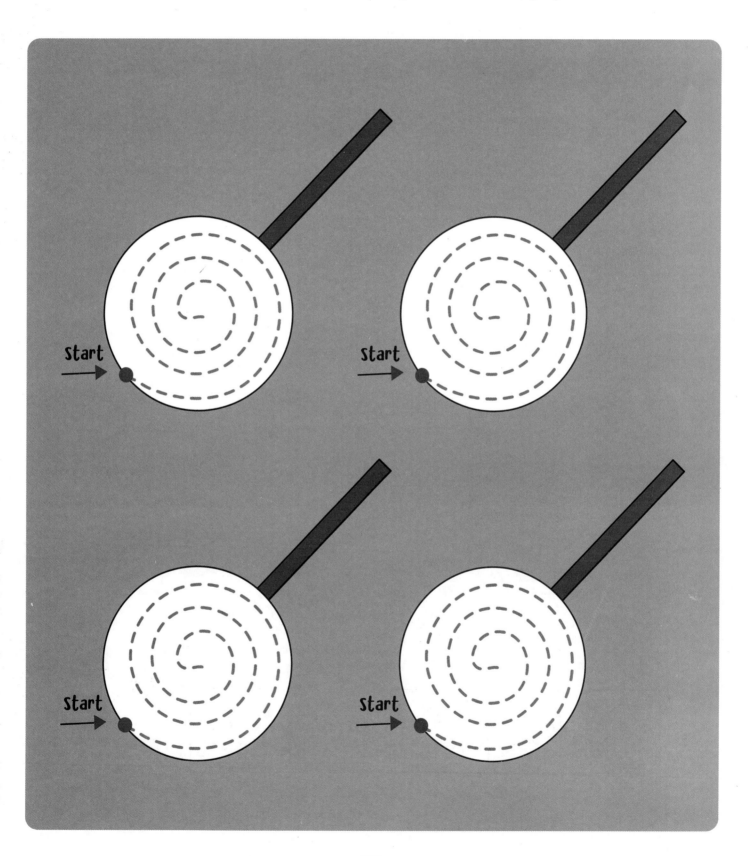

Chef's Magic

Trace the lines and complete the pattern.

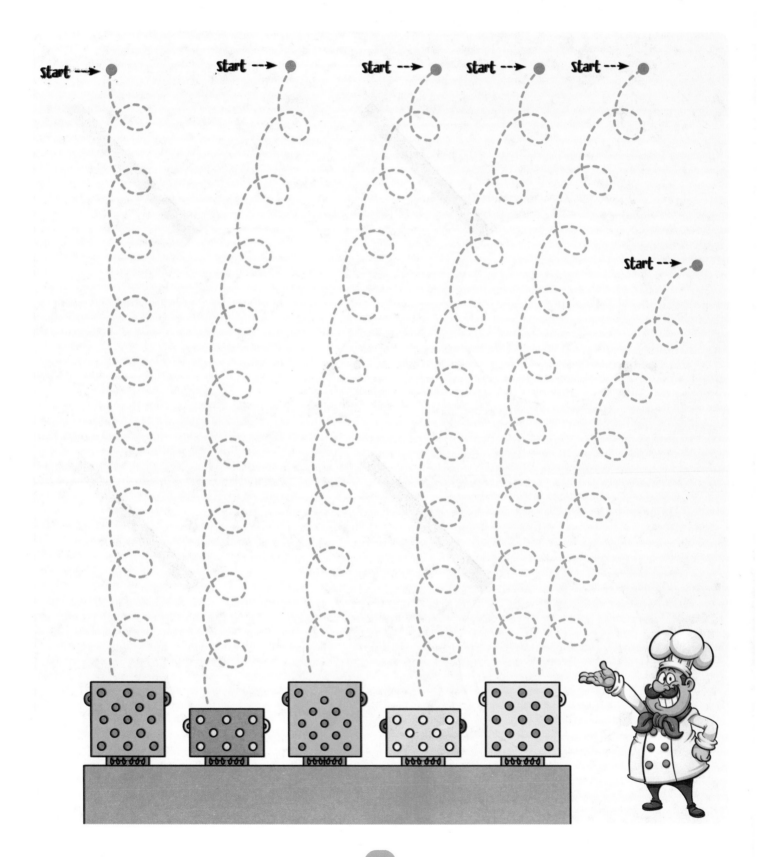

Butterfly Park

Trace the lines and complete the butterflies.

Multiple Lines

Trace the sleeping lines and color and complete the stocking.

Fun with Tracing

Identify the letter given on the left and the image on the right. Trace the line from left to right.

A is for Airplane

B is for Butterfly

C is for Cat

D is for Dinosaur

Fun with Tracing

Identify the letter given on the left and the image on the right. Trace the line from left to right.

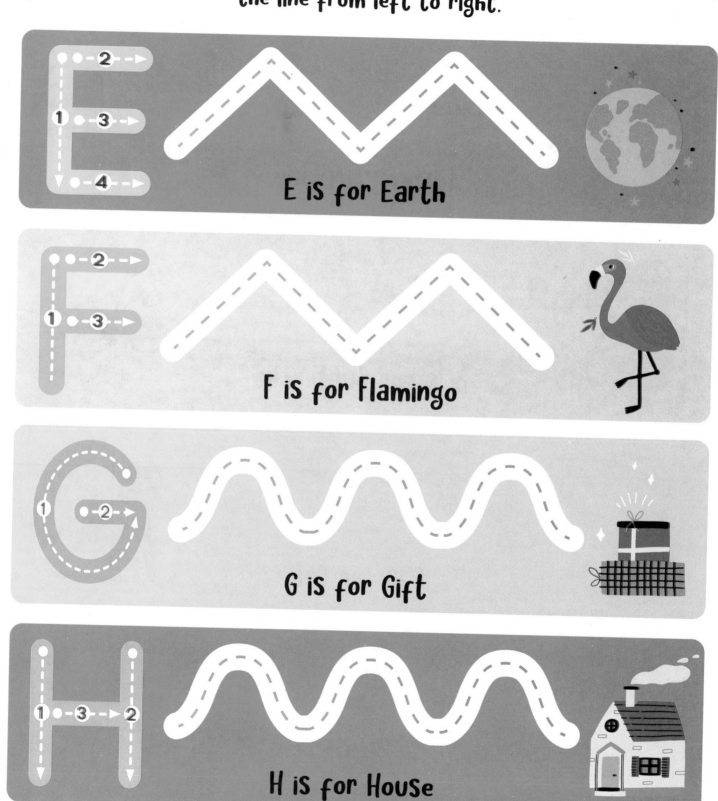

E is for Earth

F is for Flamingo

G is for Gift

H is for House

Fun with Tracing

Identify the letter given on the left and the image on the right. Trace the line from left to right.

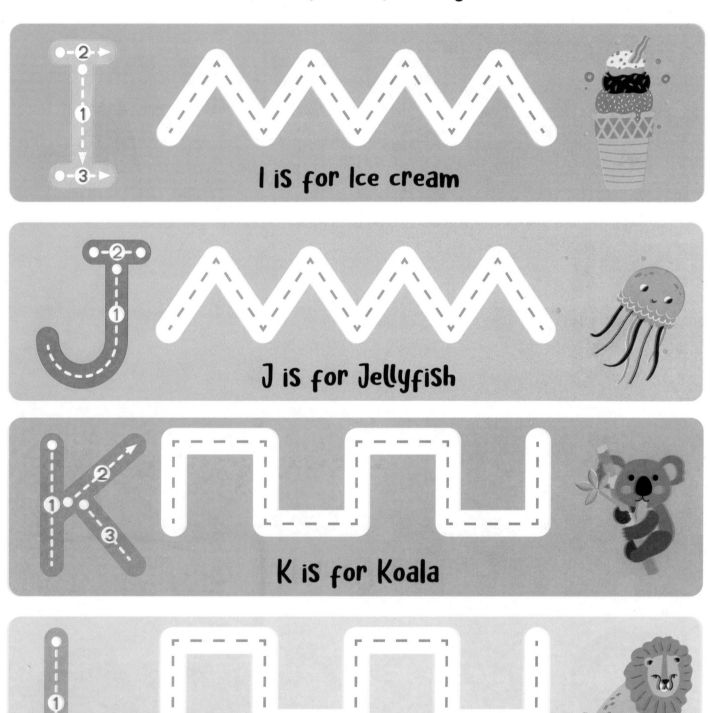

I is for Ice cream

J is for Jellyfish

K is for Koala

L is for Lion

Fun with Tracing

Identify the letter given on the left and the image on the right. Trace the line from left to right.

M is for Mountain

N is for Nose

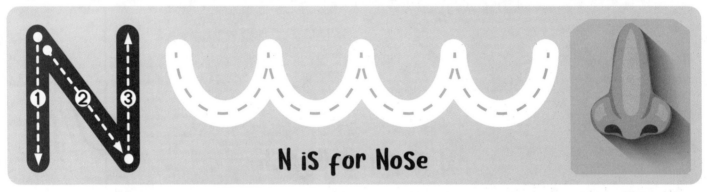

O is for Owl

P is for Pizza

Fun with Tracing

Identify the letter given on the left and the image on the right. Trace the line from left to right.

Q is for Queen

R is for Robot

S is for Snake

T is for Tree

Fun with Tracing

Identify the letter given on the left and the image on the right. Trace the line from left to right.

U is for Umbrella

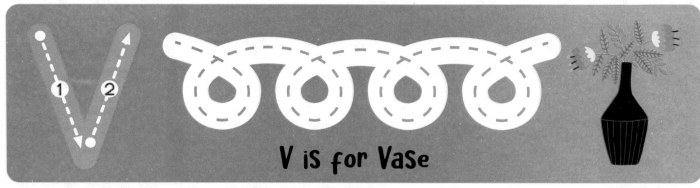

V is for Vase

W is for Watermelon

X is for Xylophone

Fun with Tracing

Identify the letter given on the left and the image on the right. Trace the line from left to right.

Y is for Yoga

Z is for Zebra

Help A reach Z by tracing the dots

Trace and write each letter.

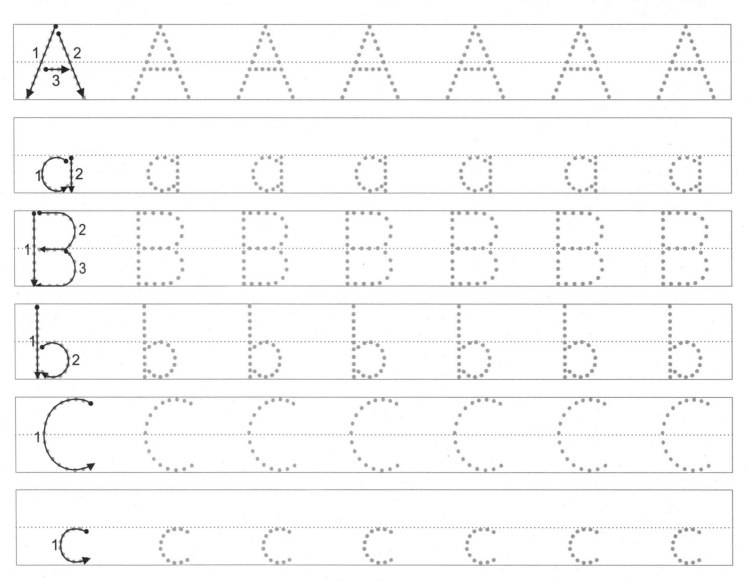

Identify these objects and write down the first letters of their names.

.... irplane   .... utterfly   .... at

28

Trace and write each letter.

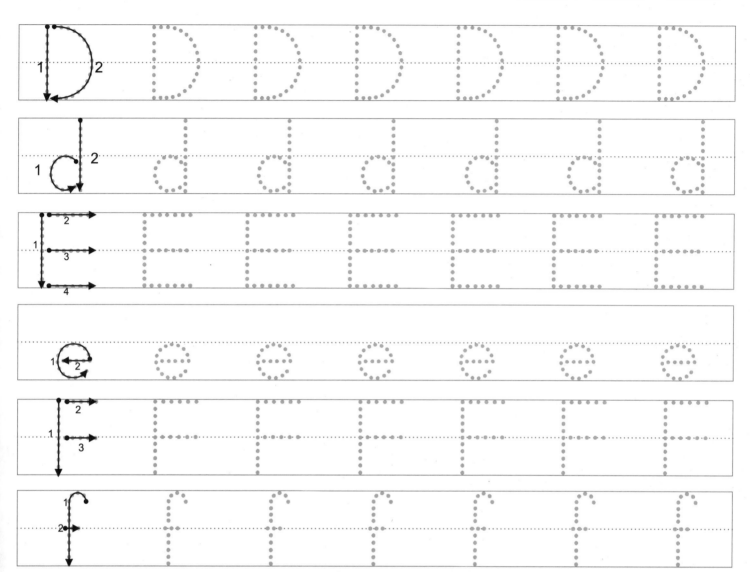

Identify these objects and write down the first letters of their names.

...... inosaur   ...... arth   ...... lamingo

Trace and write each letter.

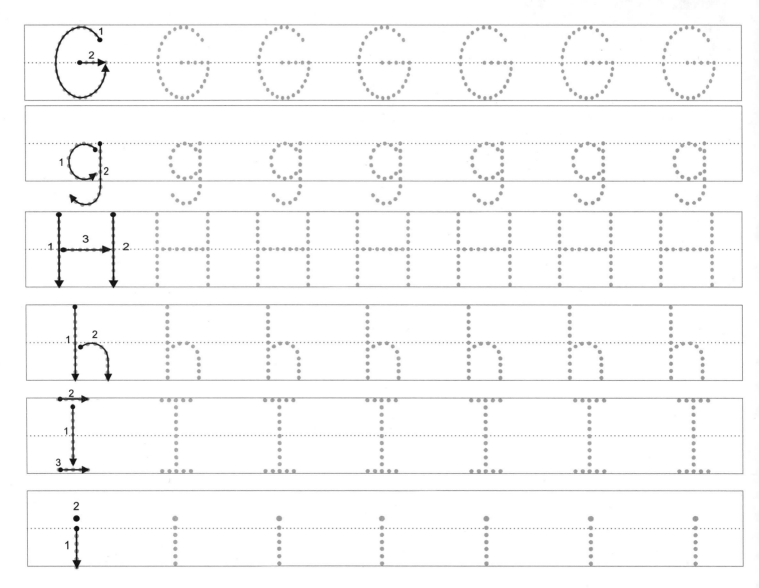

Identify these objects and write down the first letters of their names.

.... ift

.... ouse

.... ce cream

Trace and write each letter.

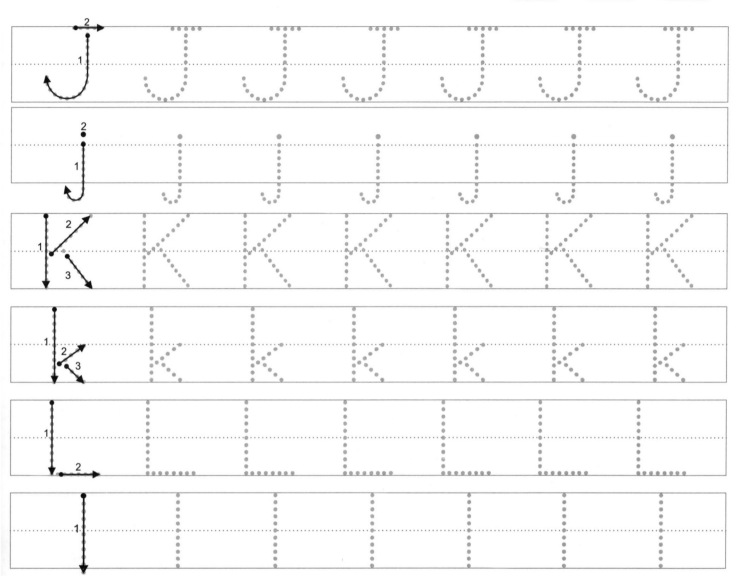

Identify these objects and write down the first letters of their names.

.... ellyfish

.... oala

.... ion

Trace and write each letter.

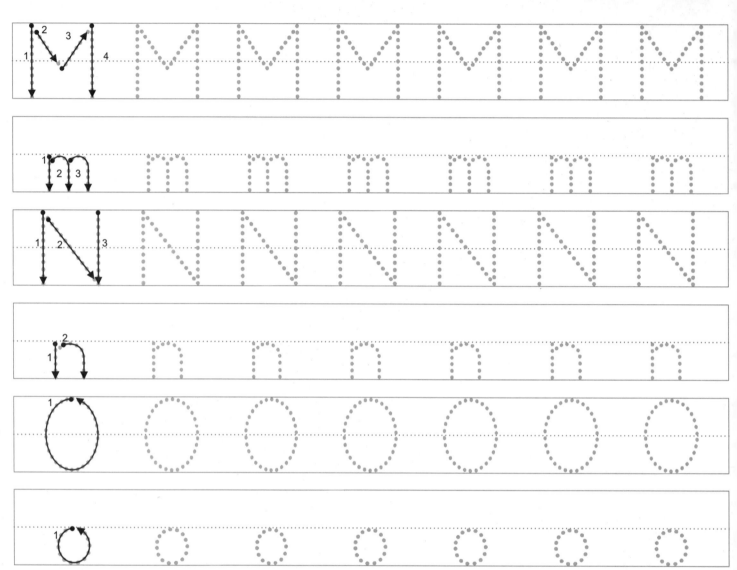

Identify these objects and write down the first letters of their names.

..... ountain   ..... oSe   ..... wl

Trace and write each letter.

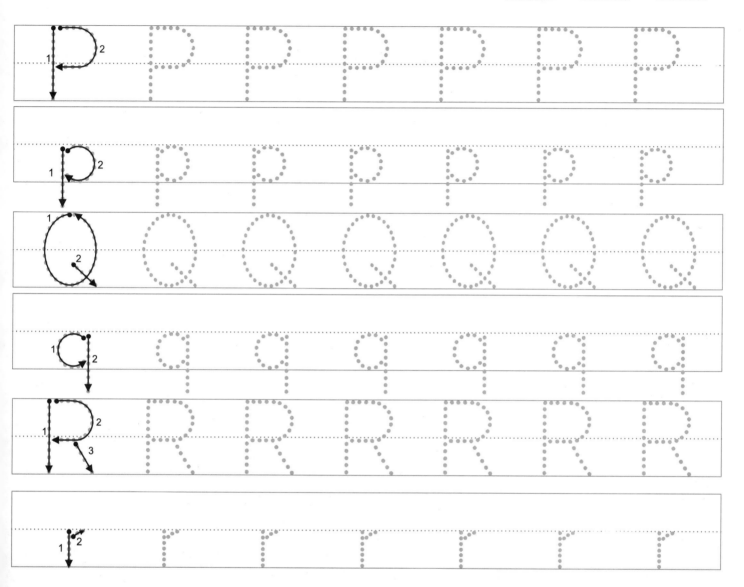

Identify these objects and write down the first letters of their names.

.......izza   ....veen   ....obot

Trace and write each letter.

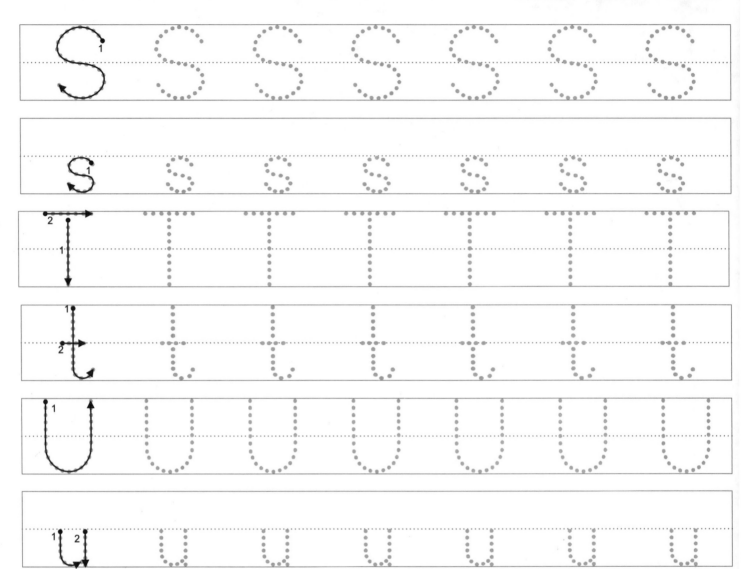

Identify these objects and write down the first letters of their names.

...... nake

.... ree

...... mbrella

Trace and write each letter.

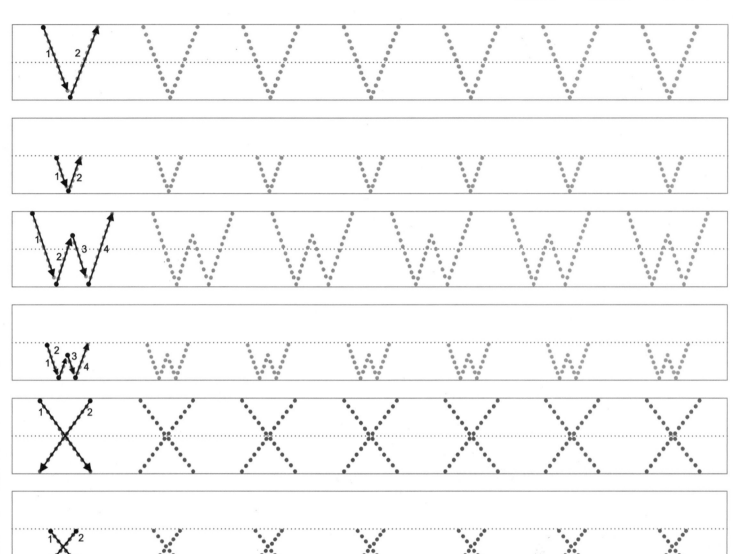

Identify these objects and write down the first letters of their names.

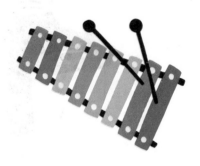

.... ase   .... atermelon   .... ylophone

Trace and write each letter.

Y Y Y Y Y Y Y

Y Y Y Y Y Y

Z Z Z Z Z Z Z

Z Z Z Z Z Z

Identify these objects and write down the first letters of their names.

.... oga

.... ebra

Three-letter name

Phonics fun with the vowel 'a'. Look at the picture and trace its three-letter name with the vowel 'a' in the middle.

cat
cat

bat
bat

fan
fan

hat
hat

b a g

b a g

c a r

c a r

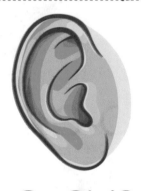

e a r

e a r

c a n

c a n

j a r

j a r

t a p

t a p

j a m

j a m

m a n

m a n

r a t

r a t

m a t

m a t

v a n

v a n

p a n

p a n

o a r

o a r

r a m

r a m

y a k

y a k

n a p

n a p

f a t

f a t

y a m

y a m

Use the picture clues to complete the three-letter words.

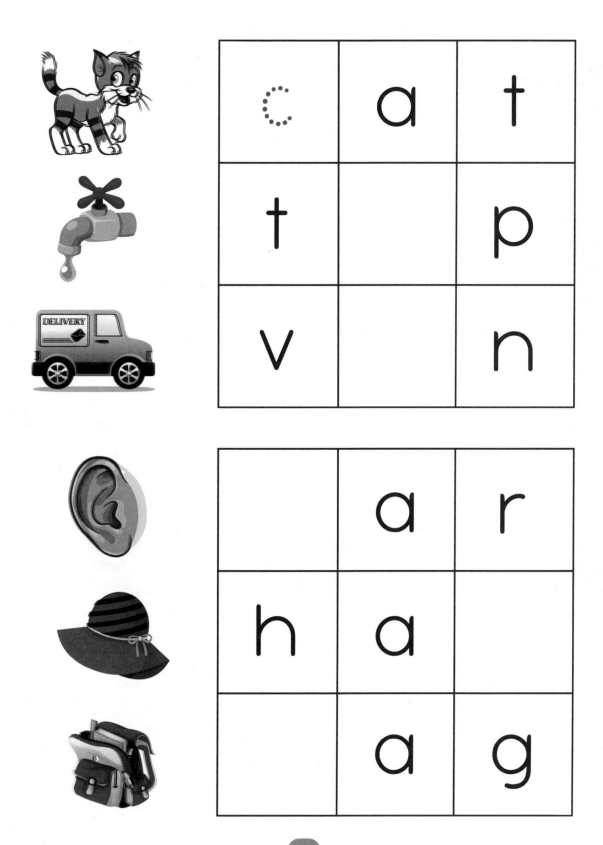

c	a	t
t		p
v		n

	a	r
h	a	
	a	g

Circle the word that matches the picture in each row and say it out loud.

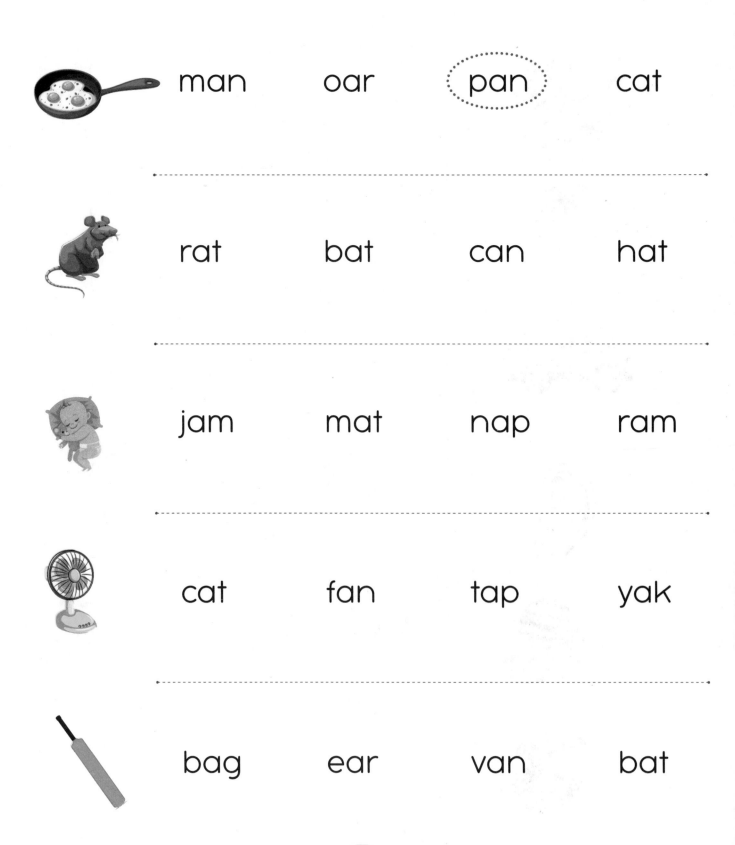

man   oar   (pan)   cat

rat   bat   can   hat

jam   mat   nap   ram

cat   fan   tap   yak

bag   ear   van   bat

Phonics fun with the vowel 'e'. Look at the pictures and trace its three-letter name with the vowel 'e' in the middle.

bee

bee

gem

gem

pen

pen

hen

hen

b e d

b e d

j e t

j e t

k e y

k e y

n e t

n e t

10

t e n

t e n

d e n

d e n

44

leg

l e g

pea

p e a

tea

t e a

web

w e b

pet

p e t

wet

w e t

dew

dew

sea

sea

eel

eel

new

new

red

red

gel

gel

Fill in the missing letters and write the words below.

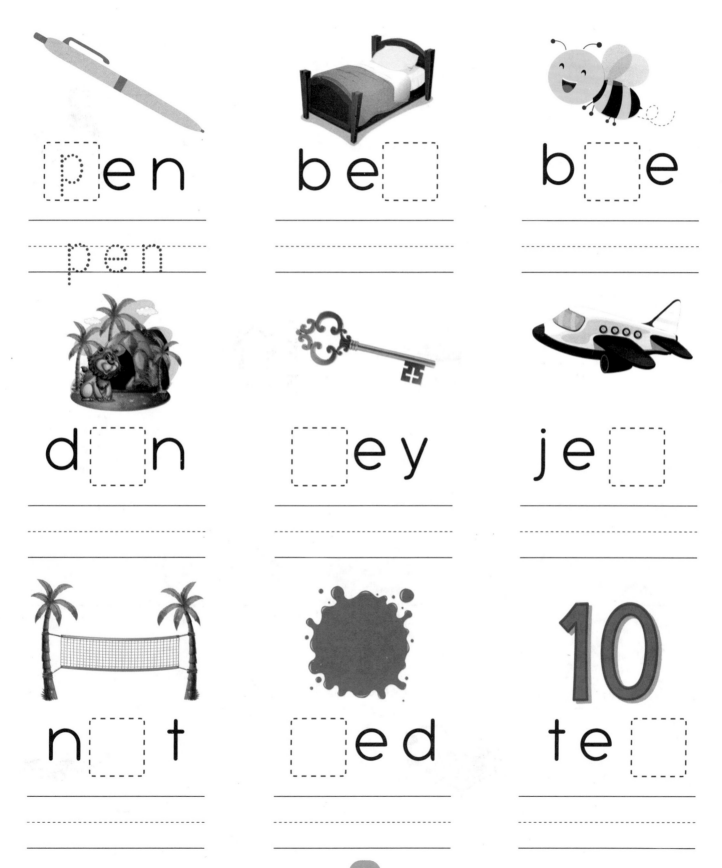

p e n

pen

b e ☐

b ☐ e

d ☐ n

☐ e y

j e ☐

n ☐ t

☐ e d

t e ☐

Using the picture clues, fill in the squares
with three-letter words.

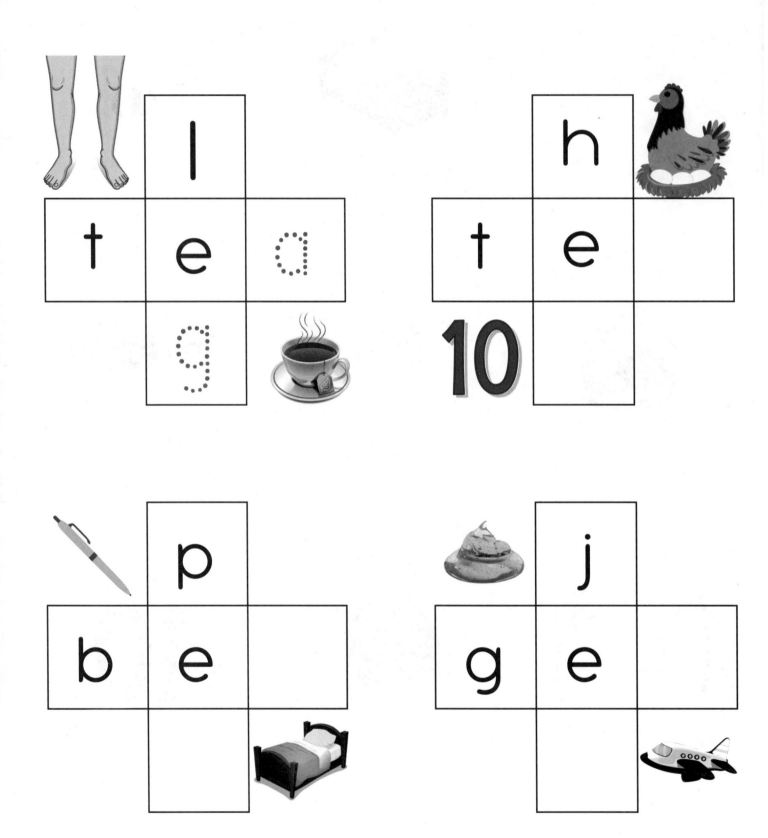

Phonics fun with the vowel ' i '. Look at the picture and trace its three-letter name with the vowel ' i ' in the middle.

pin
pin

zip
zip

pie
pie

nib
nib

bib

bib

lip

lip

fig

fig

bin

bin

sit

sit

big

big

six

six

tie

tie

lid

lid

kid

kid

oil

oil

dip

dip

air

air

dig

dig

rib

rib

win

win

kit

kit

mix

mix

Look at the pictures. Fill in the missing letters and write the words.

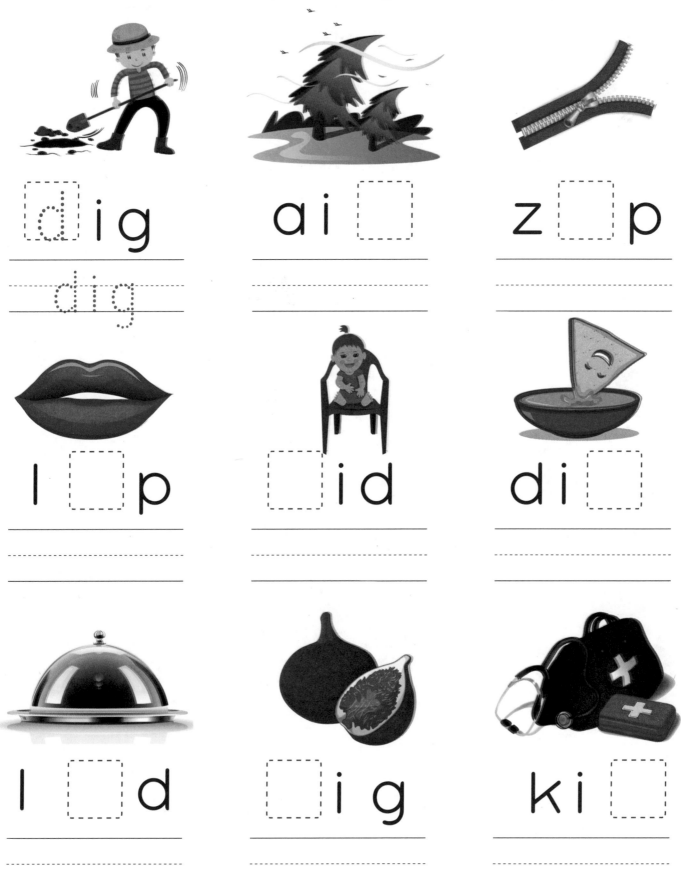

d i g

dig

a i ☐

z ☐ p

l ☐ p

☐ i d

d i ☐

l ☐ d

☐ i g

k i ☐

Unscramble the letters and write the word that matches the picture.

nip p i n

tei t i e

gfi _ i _

ikt _ i _

bni _ i _

dil _ i _

ilo _ i _

inw _ i _

ilp _ i _

dpi _ i _

piz _ i _

bib _ i _

Phonics fun with the vowel ' o '. Look at the picture and trace its three-letter name with the vowel ' o ' in the middle.

boy

boy

dog

dog

jog

jog

mop

mop

cow

cow

fox

fox

toy

toy

cot

cot

log

log

top

top

zoo

z o o

dot

dot

rot

rot

bow

bow

cop

cop

hot

hot

Phonics fun with the vowel ' U '. Look at the picture and trace its three-letter name with the vowel ' U ' in the middle.

s u n

s u n

r u n

r u n

h u t

h u t

c u p

c u p

b u g

b u g

n u t

n u t

j u g

j u g

b u s

b u s

t u b

t u b

r u g

r u g

b u d

b u d

c u b

c u b

g u m

g u m

m u d

m u d

n u n

n u n

t u g

t u g

Unscramble the letters and write the word that matches the picture.

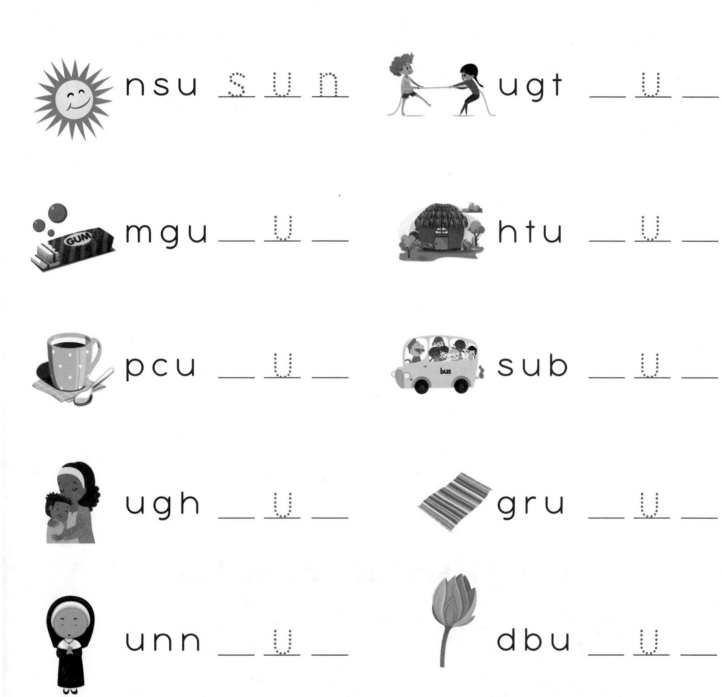

nsu   s u n

ugt   _ u _

mgu   _ u _

htu   _ u _

pcu   _ u _

sub   _ u _

ugh   _ u _

gru   _ u _

unn   _ u _

dbu   _ u _

bcu   _ u _

mdu   _ u _

Fun with Numbers

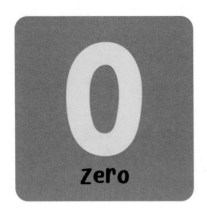

0

zero

This house has 0 windows.

Trace the number zero.

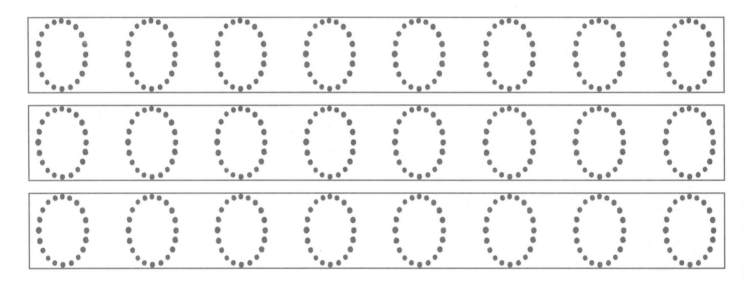

Circle the hen that has zero dots.

Fun with Numbers

Circle the house that has zero windows.

Trace the word zero.

zero zero zero zero zero

zero zero zero zero zero

Fun with Numbers

Count 1

1
one

trace the number one.

Circle the group that has one animal.

Fun with Numbers

Count the number of zebras.

trace the word one.

one one one one one

one one one one one

Fun with Numbers

two

Count 2

Trace the number two.

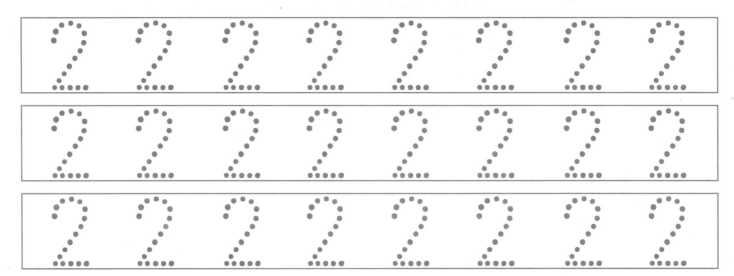

Circle the group that has two balloons.

Fun with Numbers

Count the number of Elephants.

Trace the word two.

two two two two two

two two two two two

Fun with Numbers

Count 3

three

Trace the number three.

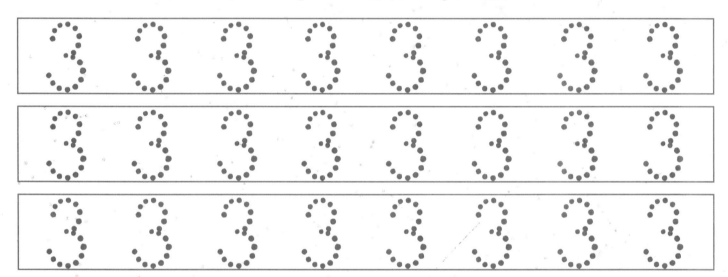

Circle the basket that has three fruits.

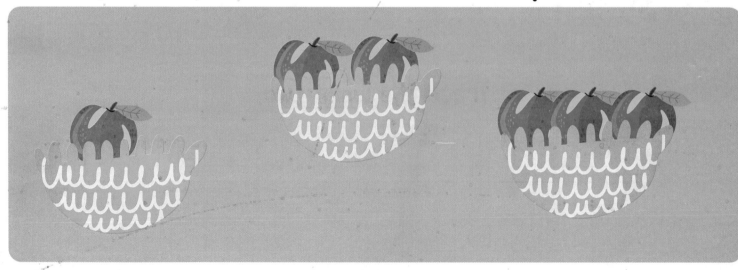

Fun with Numbers

Count the number of fish.

Trace the word three.

three	three	three	three

three	three	three	three

Fun with Numbers

Count 4

Trace the number four.

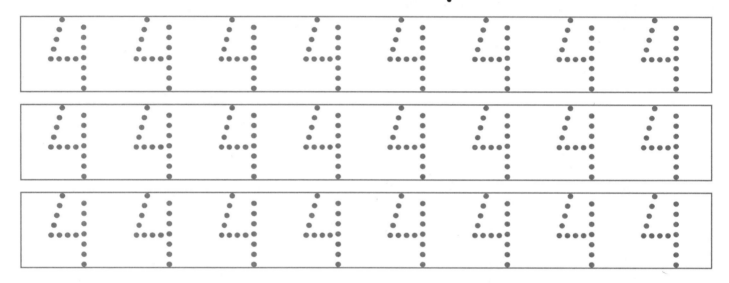

Circle the nest that has four birds.

Fun with Numbers

Count the number of lions.

Trace the word four.

four   four   four   four

four   four   four   four

Fun with Numbers

five

Count 5

Trace the number five.

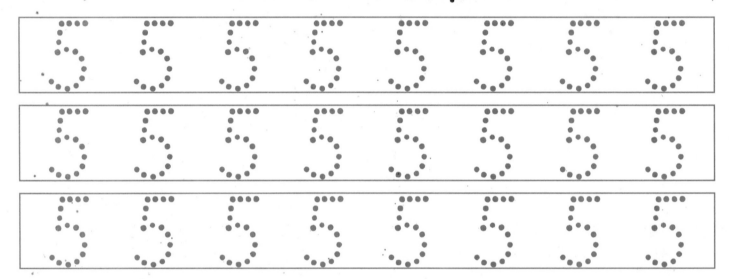

Circle the bug that has five dots.

Fun with Numbers

Count the number of koalas.

Trace the word five.

five   five   five   five

five   five   five   five

Fun with Numbers

Count 6

Trace the number Six.

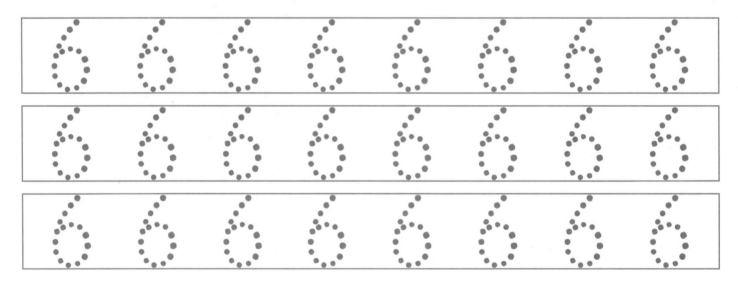

Circle the pot that has six fishes.

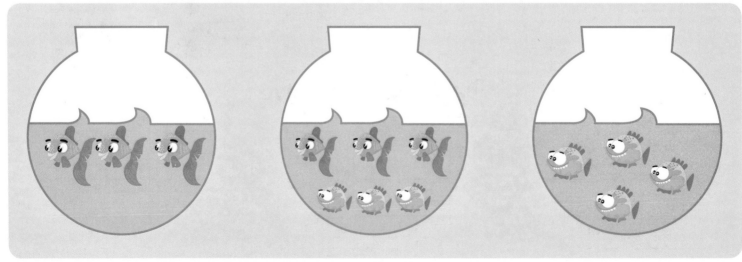

Fun with Numbers

Count the number of pandas.

Trace the word Six.

six	six	six	six

six	six	six	six

Fun with Numbers

Count 7

Trace the number Seven.

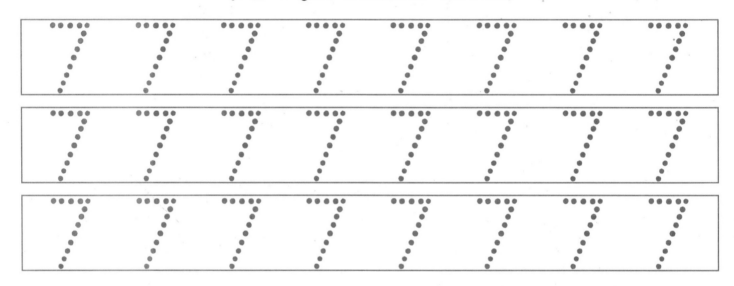

Circle the tree that has Seven fruits.

Fun with Numbers

Count the number of butterflies.

Trace the word Seven.

Seven Seven Seven Seven

Seven Seven Seven Seven

Fun with Numbers

Count 8

8
eight

Trace the number eight.

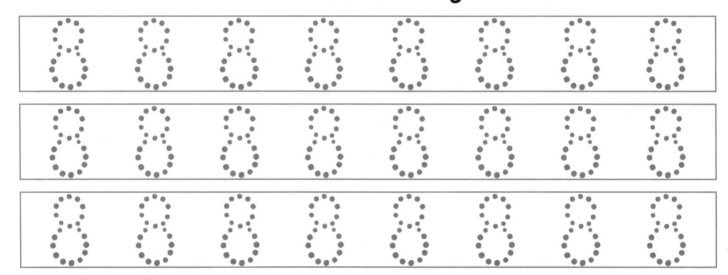

Circle the vase that has eight flowers.

Fun with Numbers

Count the number of foxes.

Trace the word eight.

eight   eight   eight   eight

eight   eight   eight   eight

Fun with Numbers

nine

Trace the number nine.

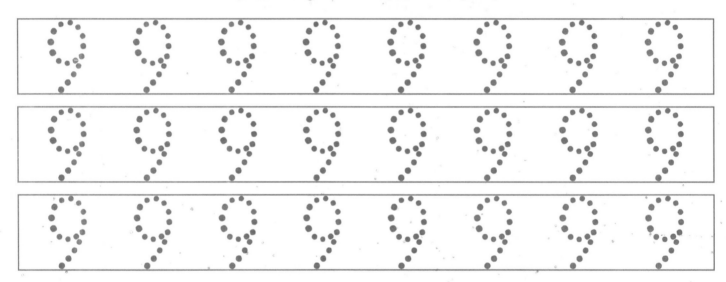

Circle the group that has nine butterflies.

Fun with Numbers

Count the number of skunks.

Trace the word nine.

nine   nine   nine   nine

nine   nine   nine   nine

Fun with Numbers

Count 10

ten

Trace the number ten.

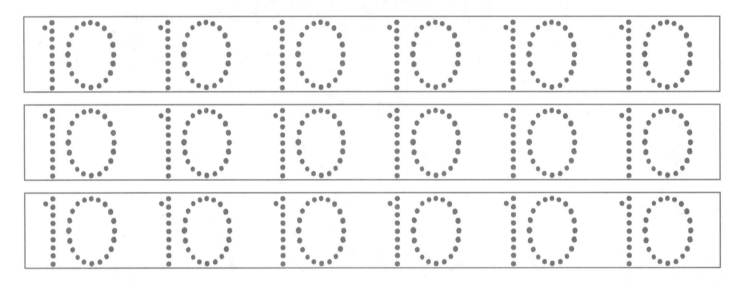

Circle the group that has ten honey bees.

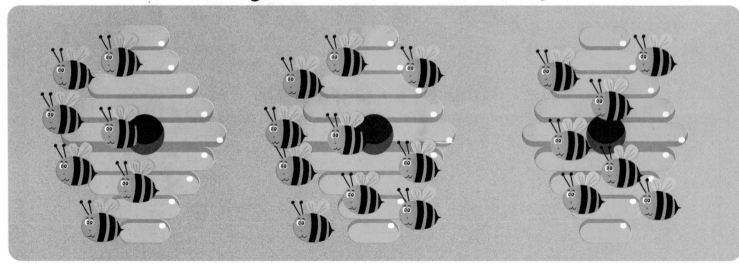

Fun with Numbers

Count the number of octopuses.

Trace the word ten.

ten ten ten ten ten ten

ten ten ten ten ten ten

Connect the dots and color the picture.

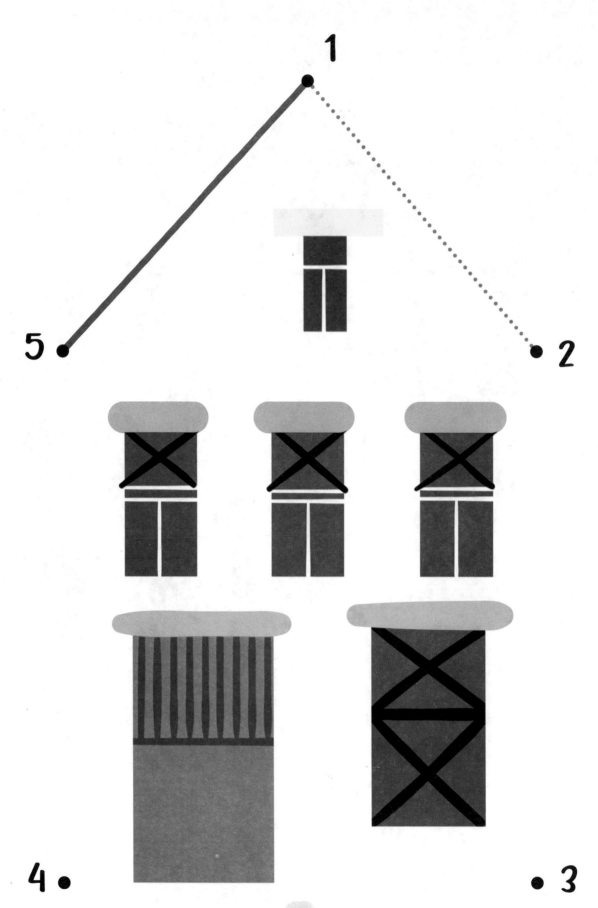

Count, Color and Write

Count the objects given on the left and color the same number of circles.
Write the number in the box given on the right.

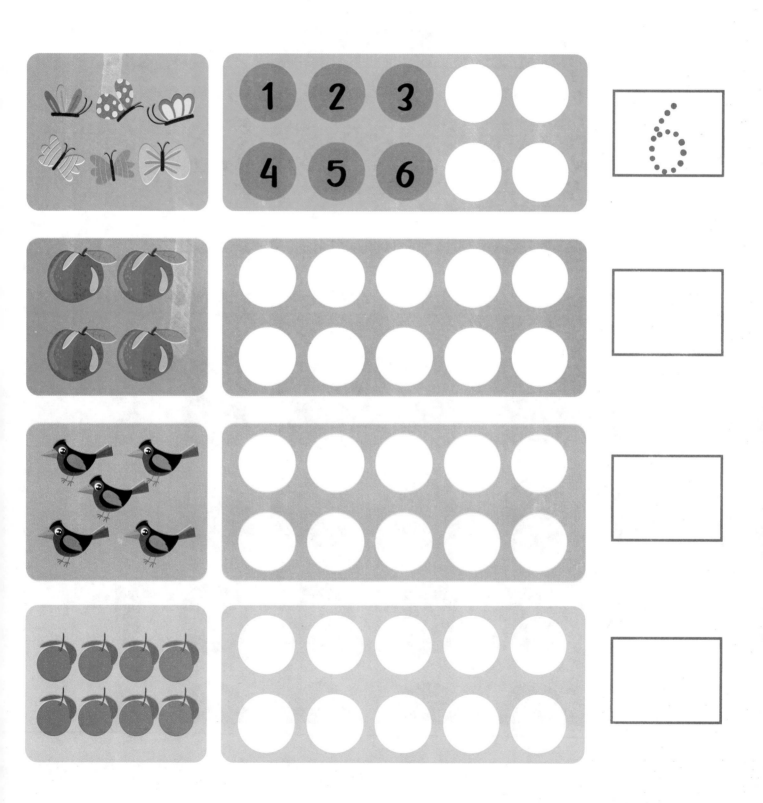

Connect the dots and color the picture.

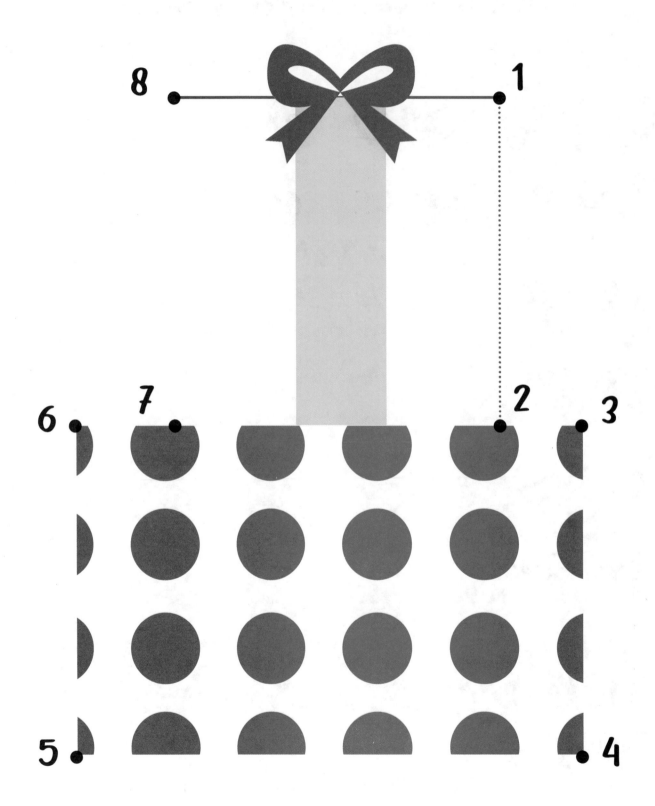

Count, Color and Write

Count the objects given on the left and color the same number of circles.
Write the number in the box given on the right.

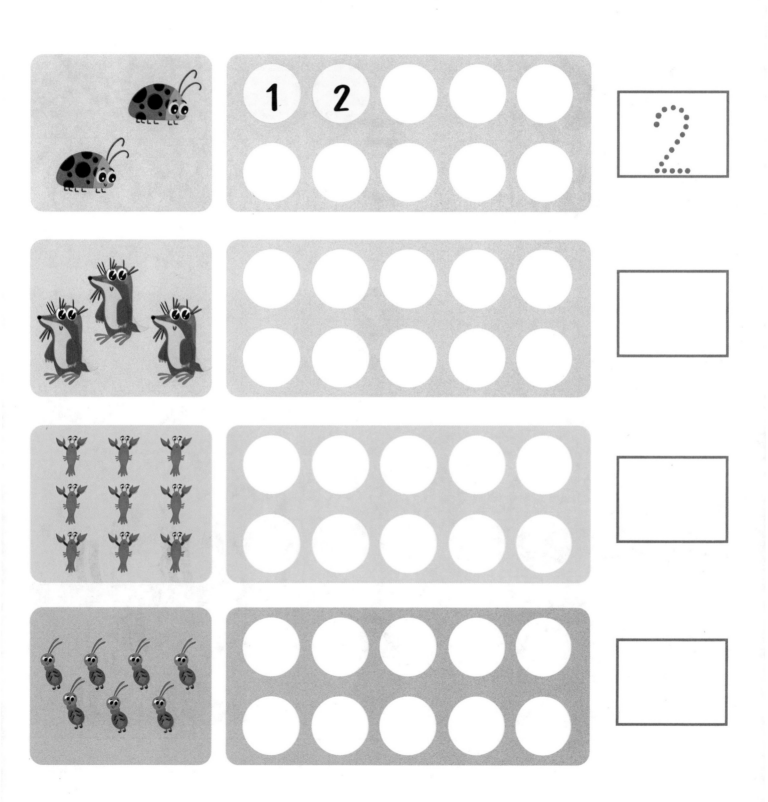

Fun with Counting

Count the objects given in the box and write the answer in the space given below. Take a cue from the given numbers.

5

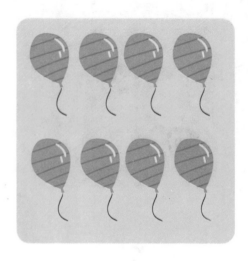

9

....

....

4

8

....

....

Fun with Counting

Count the objects given in the box and write the answer in the space given below. Take a cue from the given numbers.

6

9

....

....

7

3

....

....

Fun with Numbers

Count the airplanes

11

eleven

Trace the number eleven.

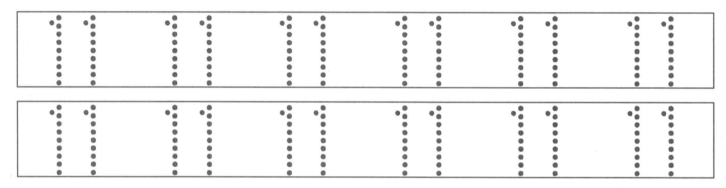

Circle the plate that has 11 fruits.

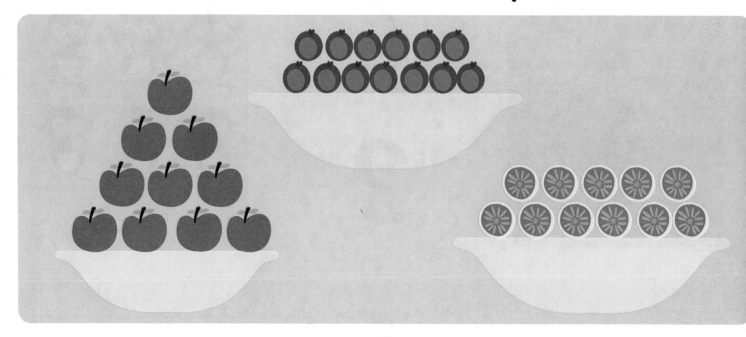

Fun with Numbers

Count the sailboats.

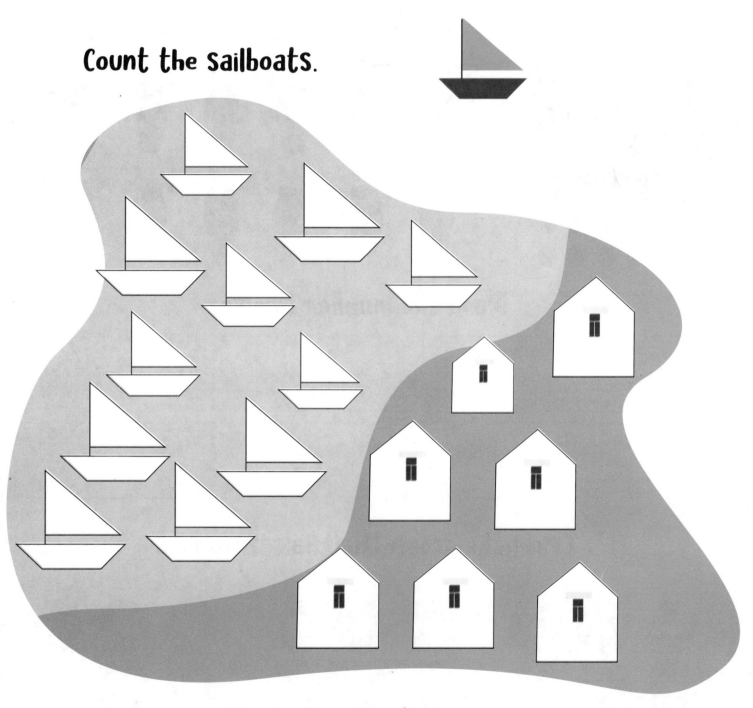

Trace the word eleven.

eleven   eleven   eleven

eleven   eleven   eleven

Fun with Numbers

Count the ice creams.

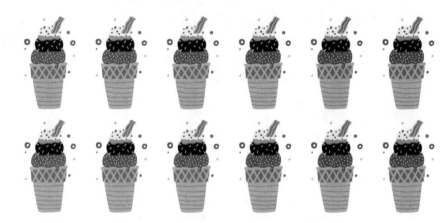

Trace the number twelve.

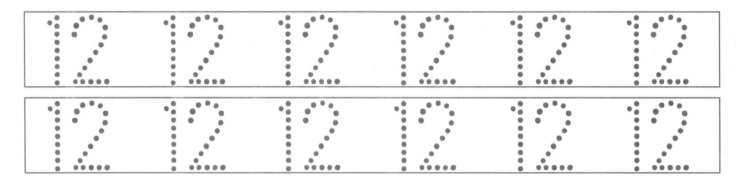

Circle the group that has 12 donuts.

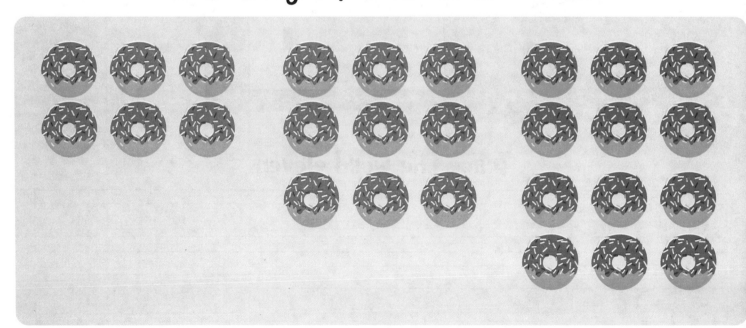

Fun with Numbers

Count the cups.

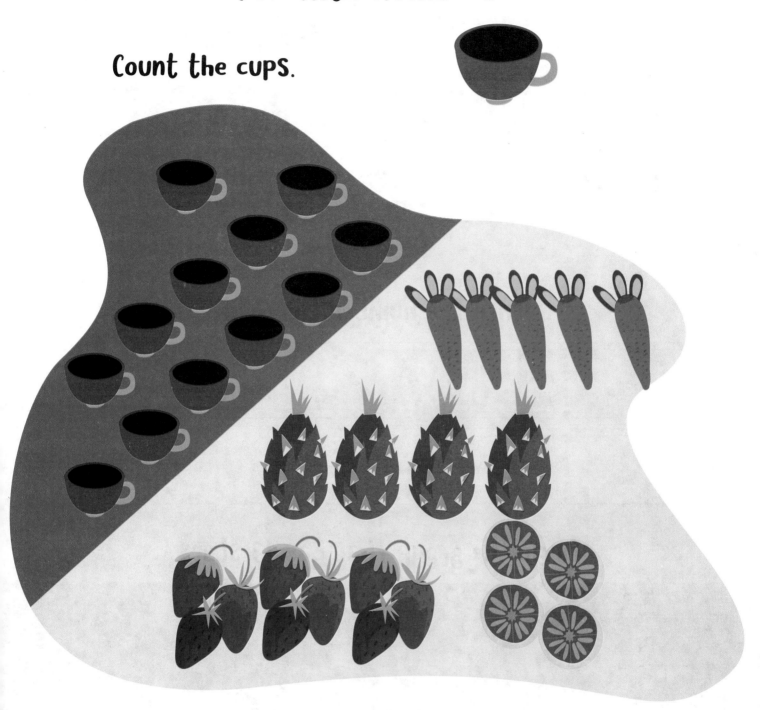

Trace the word twelve.

twelve   twelve   twelve

twelve   twelve   twelve

Fun with Numbers

Count the dolphins.

13

thirteen

Trace the number thirteen.

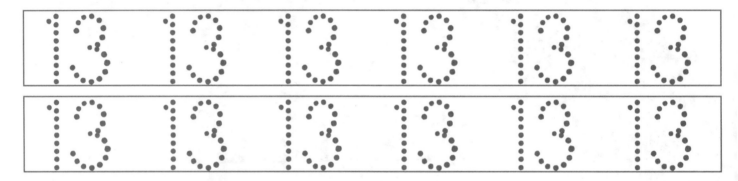

Circle the group that has 13 stars.

Fun with Numbers

Count and color these fish.

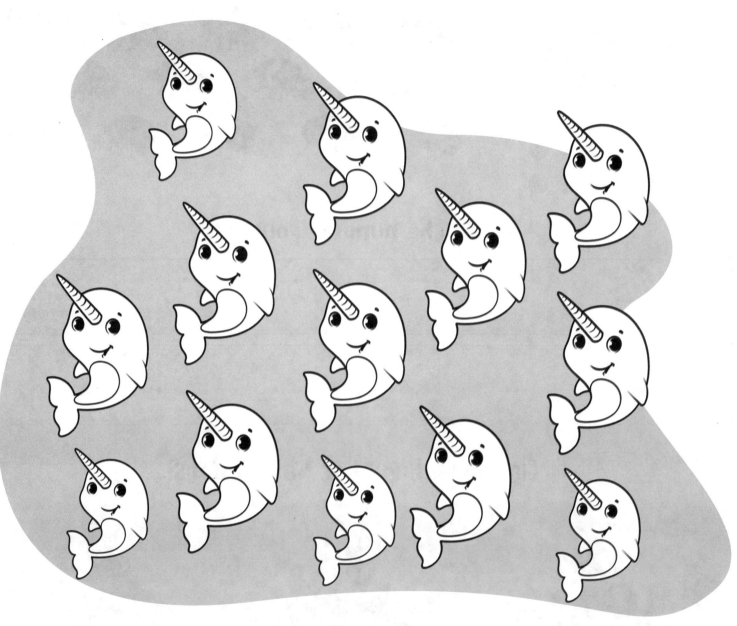

Trace the word thirteen.

thirteen thirteen thirteen

thirteen thirteen thirteen

Fun with Numbers

14
fourteen

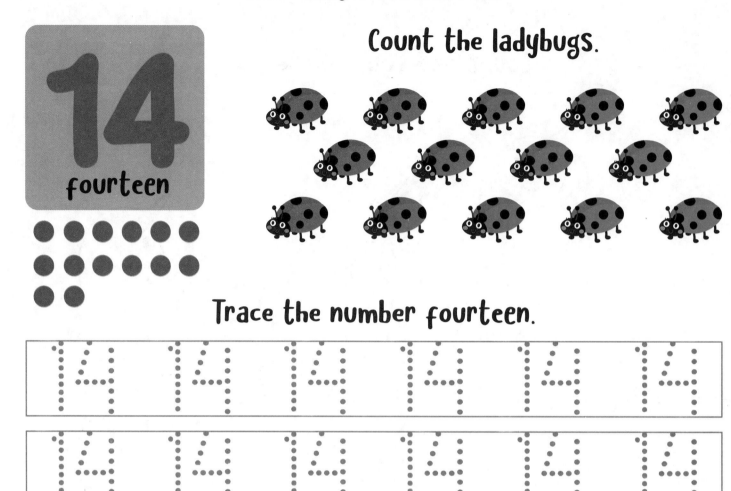

Count the ladybugs.

Trace the number fourteen.

14 14 14 14 14 14

14 14 14 14 14 14

Circle the bug that has 14 dots.

Fun with Numbers

Join the dots and color the picture.

Trace the word fourteen.

fourteen fourteen fourteen

fourteen fourteen fourteen

Fun with Numbers

15

fifteen

Count the dragonflies.

Trace the number fifteen.

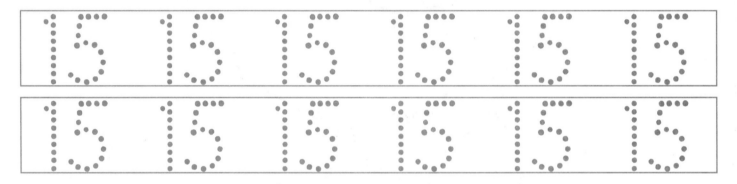

Circle the group that has 15 flowers.

Fun with Numbers

Join the dots and color the picture.

Trace the word fifteen.

fifteen   fifteen   fifteen

fifteen   fifteen   fifteen

Fun with Numbers

16
sixteen

Count the butterflies.

Trace the number sixteen.

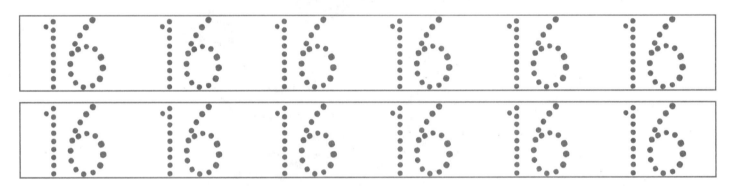

Circle the owl that has 16 feathers.

Fun with Numbers

Join the dots and color the picture.

Trace the word sixteen.

sixteen	sixteen	sixteen

sixteen	sixteen	sixteen

Fun with Numbers

17
Seventeen

Count the ants.

Trace the number Seventeen.

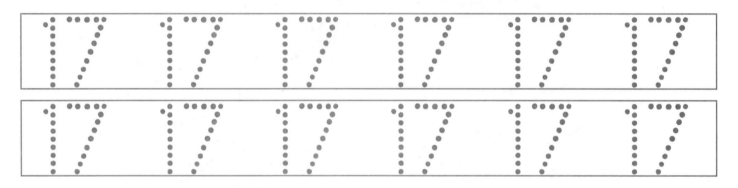

Circle the pot that has 17 marbles.

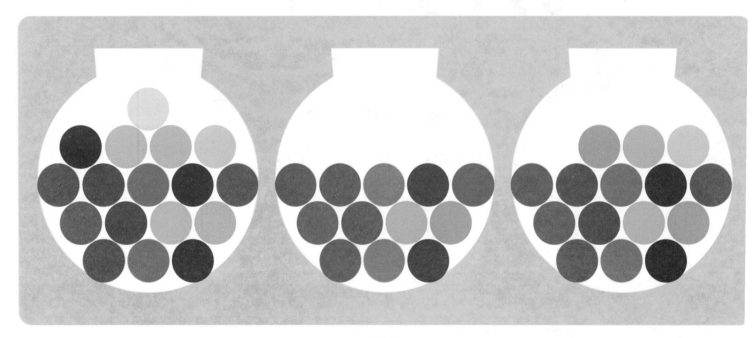

Fun with Numbers

Join the dots and color the picture.

Trace the word seventeen.

seventeen   seventeen

seventeen   seventeen

Fun with Counting

Count the objects given in the box and write the answer in the space given below. Take a cue from the given numbers.

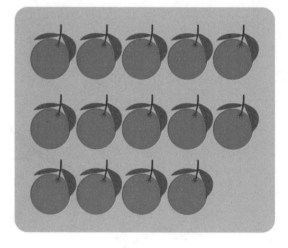

11

12

.... 12 ....

....

13

14

....

....

Fun with Counting

Count the objects given in the box and write the answer in the space given below. Take a cue from the given numbers.

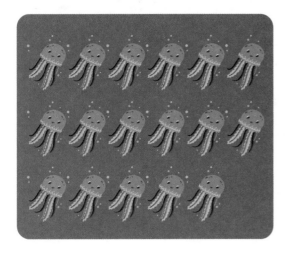

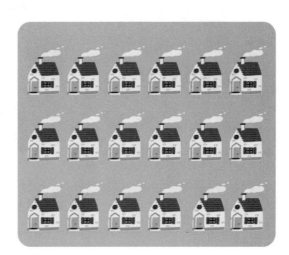

16

15

....

....

17

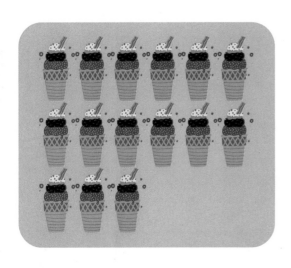

18

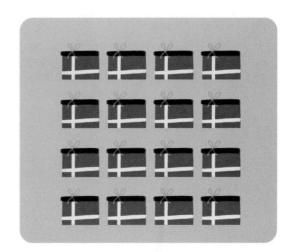

....

....

Fun with Numbers

18
eighteen

Count the strawberries.

Trace the number eighteen.

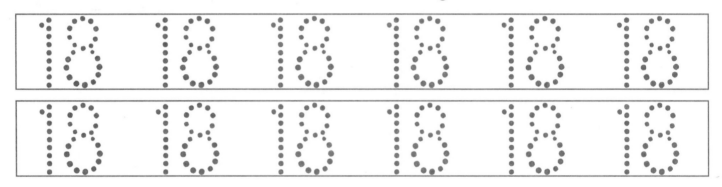

Circle the umbrella that has 18 dots.

Fun with Numbers

Join the dots and color the picture.

Trace the word eighteen.

eighteen eighteen eighteen

eighteen eighteen eighteen

Fun with Numbers

19
nineteen

Count the butterflies.

Trace the number nineteen.

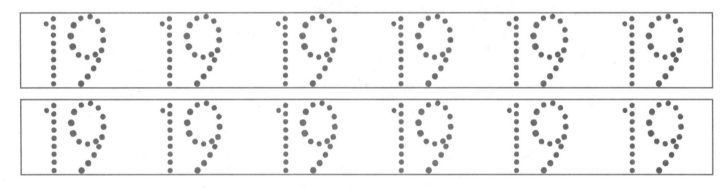

Circle the group that has 19 trees.

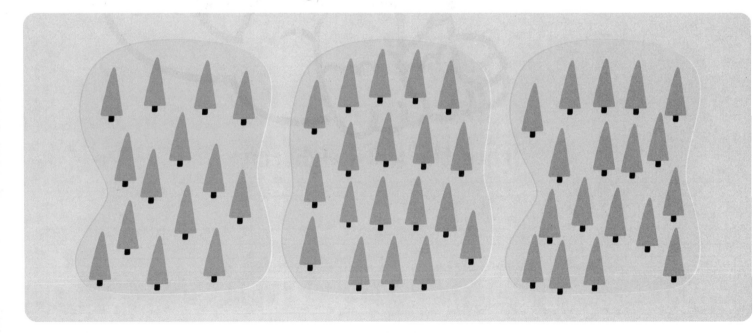

Fun with Numbers

Join the dots and color the picture.

Trace the word nineteen.

nineteen nineteen nineteen

nineteen nineteen nineteen

Fun with Numbers

Count the birds.

20

twenty

Trace the number twenty.

20 20 20 20 20

20 20 20 20 20

Circle the group that has 20 mushrooms.

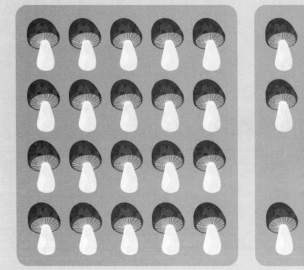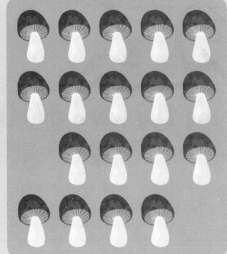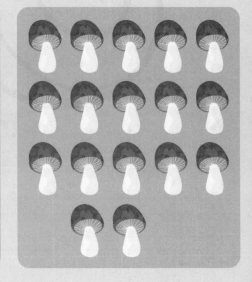

Fun with Numbers

Join the dots and color the picture.

Trace the word twenty.

twenty   twenty   twenty

twenty   twenty   twenty

Count, Color and Write

Count the objects given on the left and color the same number of circles.
Write the number in the box given on the right.

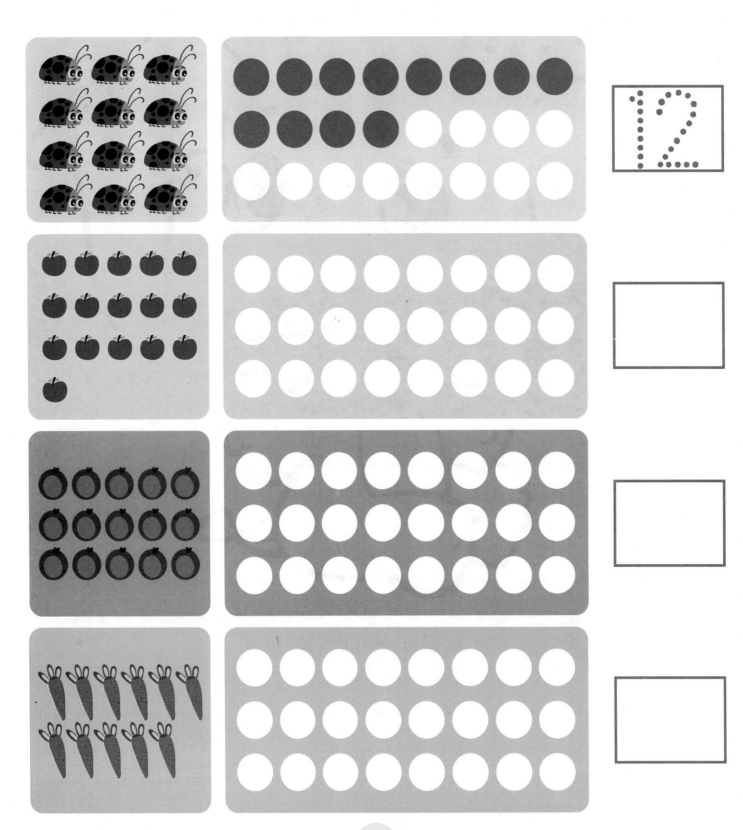

Count, Color and Write

Count the objects given on the left and color the same number of circles.
Write the number in the box given on the right.

Addition

Count the objects and add them. Write the total number in the box.

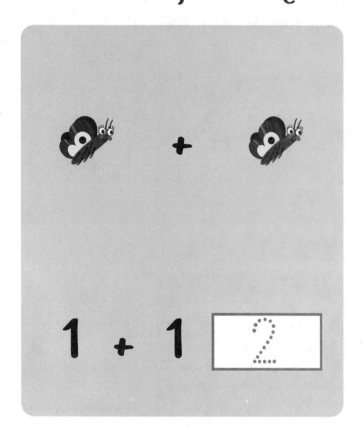

1 + 1 = 2

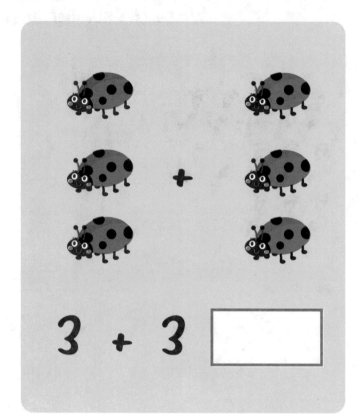

3 + 3 =

2 + 1 =

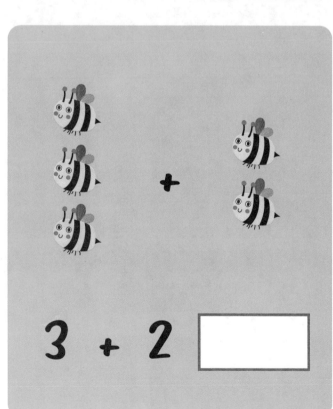

3 + 2 =

Addition

Count the objects and add them. Write the total number in the box.

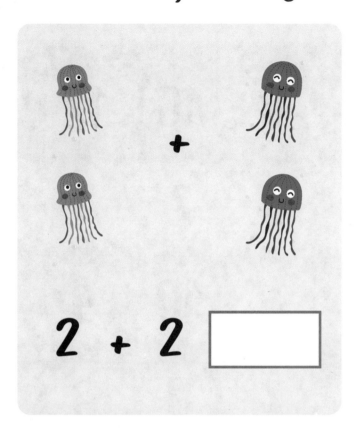

2 + 2 ☐

3 + 1 ☐

2 + 2 ☐

4 + 1 ☐

Follow the numbers and trace the path from 1-20.

Missing Numbers

Observe the pattern and write the missing numbers in the circles given below.

1 2 3 4 5
___ 7 8 9 ___
11 ___ 13 14 15
16 ___ 18 19 ___

Write the missing middle number in the box.

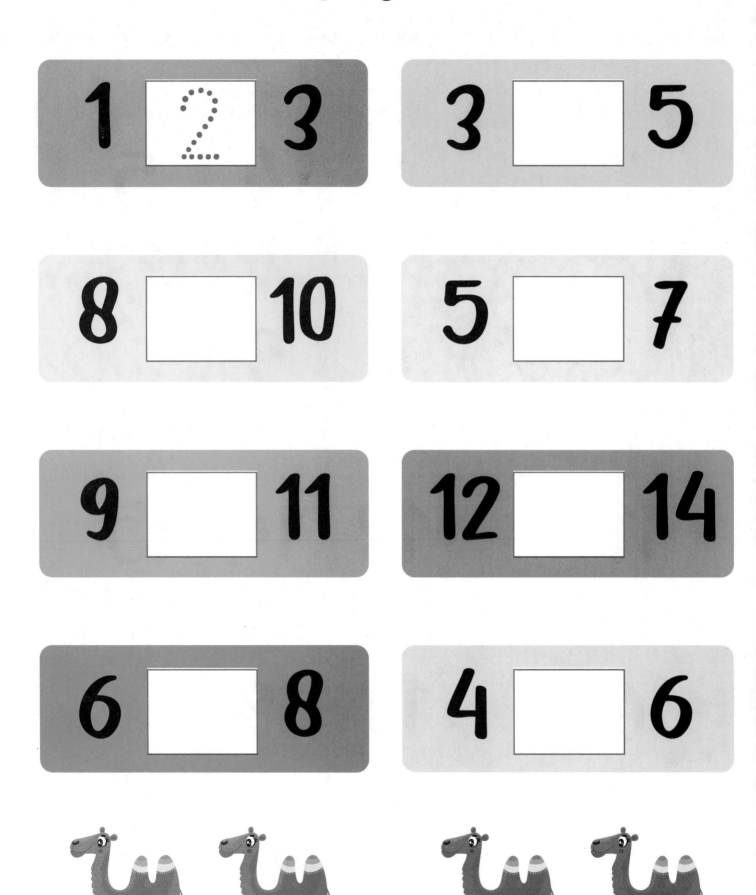

1 [2] 3

3 [ ] 5

8 [ ] 10

5 [ ] 7

9 [ ] 11

12 [ ] 14

6 [ ] 8

4 [ ] 6

Write the missing middle number in the box.

| 2 | 3 | 4 |

| 10 | | 12 |

| 14 | | 16 |

| 15 | | 17 |

| 16 | | 18 |

| 17 | | 19 |

| 13 | | 15 |

| 18 | | 20 |

Help Little Red Riding Hood reach her house by following the numbers from 1-20.

Help Little Bunny reach her carrots by following the numbers from 1–20.

Write the number that comes after.

1 2 3

3 comes after
1 and 2.

1 2 [3]

4 5 [ ]

6 7 [ ]

8 9 [ ]

2 3 [ ]

3 4 [ ]

7 8 [ ]

9 10 [ ]

Write the number that comes before.

1 2 3

1 comes before
2 and 3.

3 | 4 5

☐ | 3 4

☐ | 8 9

☐ | 6 7

☐ | 2 3

☐ | 5 6

☐ | 9 10

☐ | 7 8

Which Number is Greater?

Count each object given in the box and circle the greater number.

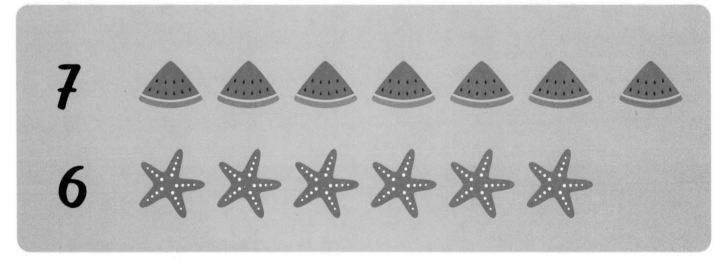

Which Number is Greater?

Count each object given in the box and circle the greater number.

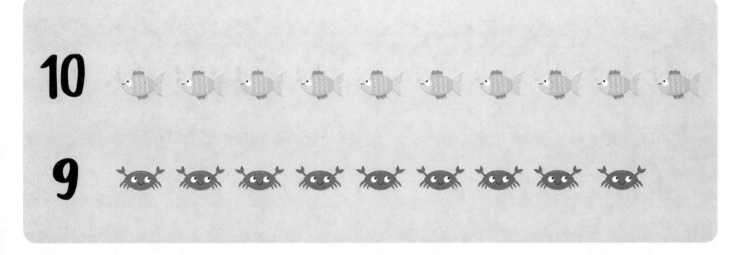

Which Number is Lesser?

Count each object given in the box and circle the number that is Lesser.

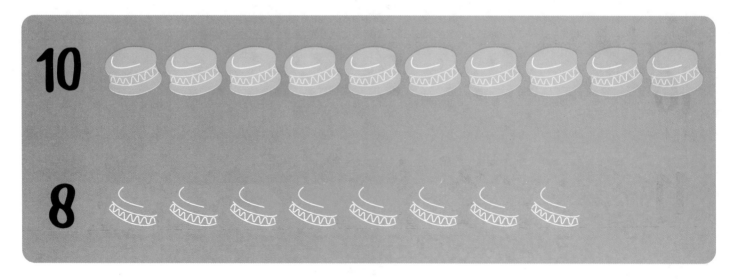

Which Number is Lesser?

Count each object given in the box and circle the number that is Lesser.

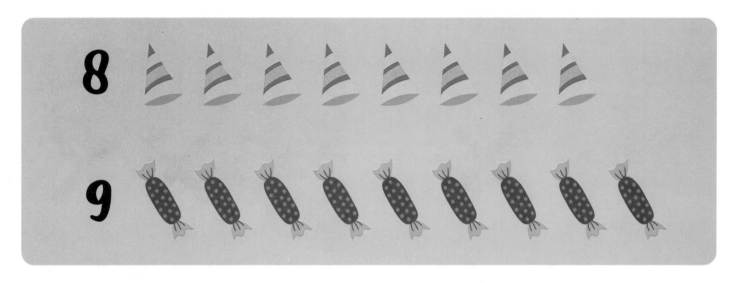

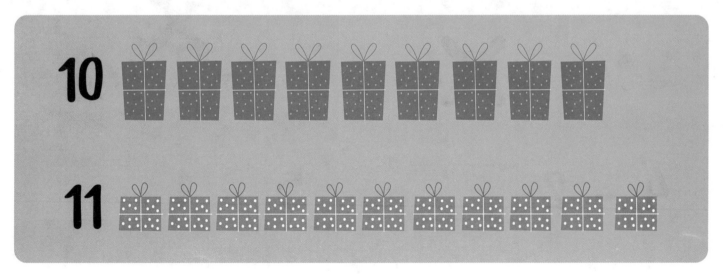

Subtraction

Count the objects and subtract the ones that are crossed out.
Write the answer in the box.

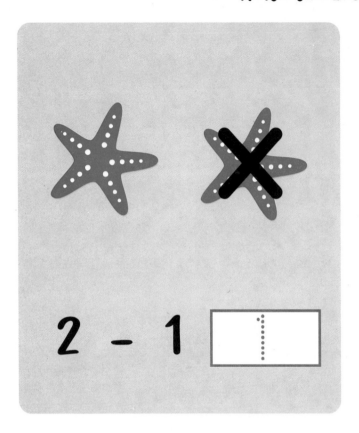

2 - 1 [1]

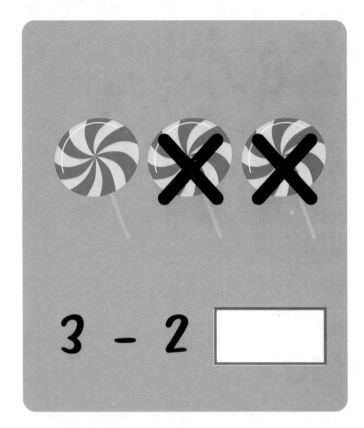

3 - 2 [ ]

4 - 2 [ ]

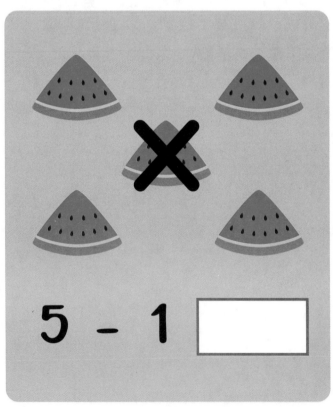

5 - 1 [ ]

Subtraction

Count the objects and subtract the ones that are crossed out.
Write the answer in the box.

6 – 2

6 – 3

4 – 3

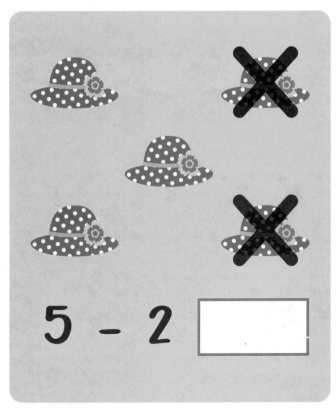

5 – 2

Subtraction

Count the objects and subtract the ones that are crossed out.
Write the answer in the box.

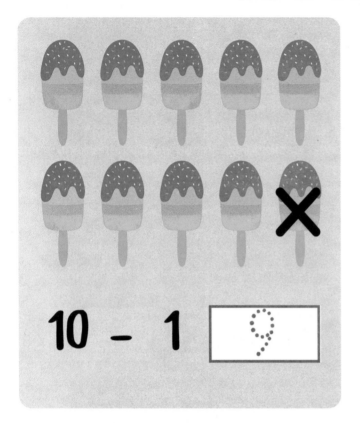

10 – 1   9

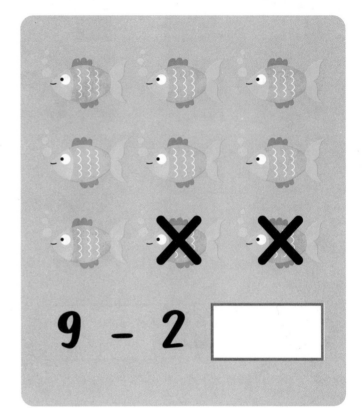

9 – 2

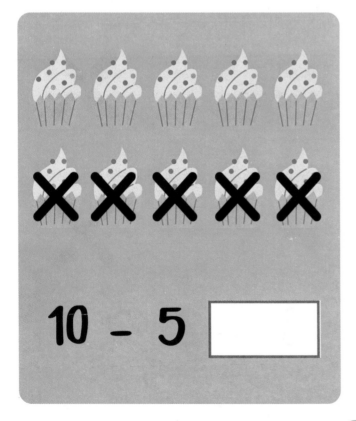

10 – 5

18 – 1

Subtraction

Count the objects and subtract the ones that are crossed out.
Write the answer in the box.

15 – 5 ☐

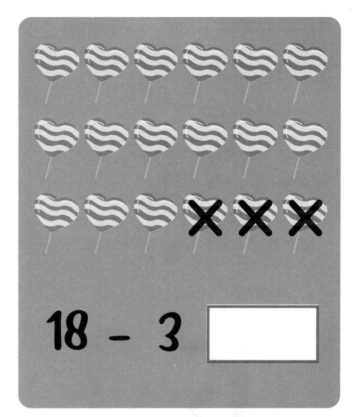

18 – 3 ☐

15 – 2 ☐

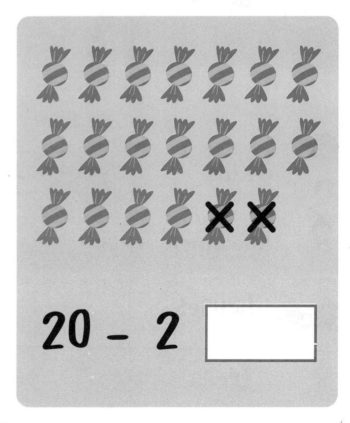

20 – 2 ☐

Learn with Graphs!

Count the number of objects and color the graph accordingly.

	1	2	3	4	5
Kids	▨	▨	▨	▨	▨
Snowmen					
houses					
trees					

Learn with Graphs!

Count the number of objects and color the graph accordingly.

	1	2	3	4	5
Starfish					
Octopuses					
fish					
Sharks					

 Starfish

 Octopuses

fish

Sharks

Learn with Graphs!

Count the number of objects and color the graph accordingly.

	1	2	3	4	5
horses	▨	▨	▨		
clowns					
canons					
elephants					

Learn with Graphs!

Count the number of objects and color the graph accordingly.

	1	2	3	4	5

 cycles

 boats

 houses

birds

Drawing Shapes

Draw these shapes by connecting the dots.

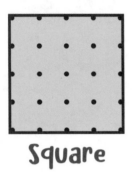

Square

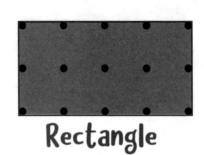

Rectangle

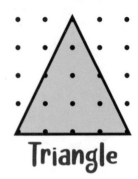

Triangle

Draw a square

Draw a rectangle

Draw a triangle

Draw another triangle

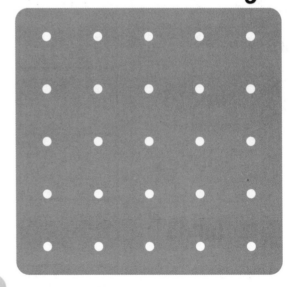

Color by Shape

Trace the dots to draw the shapes given below. Fill in the matching color.

Finding Shapes

Count the number of each Shape in the picture given below and write down the answers in the blanks.

● ....   ▲ ....   ⬜ ....   ⬜ ....

Finding Shapes

Count the number of each shape in the picture given below and write down the answers in the blanks.

● .... ▲ .... ▭ .... ◼ ....

Finding Shapes

Count the number of each Shape in the picture given below and write down the answers in the blanks.

Finding Shapes

Count the number of each Shape in the picture given below and write down the answers in the blanks.

● .... ▲ .... ▭ .... ▢ ....

Shapes and Sides

Trace the dots to draw a shape. Count the number of sides in each shape and write the answer below.

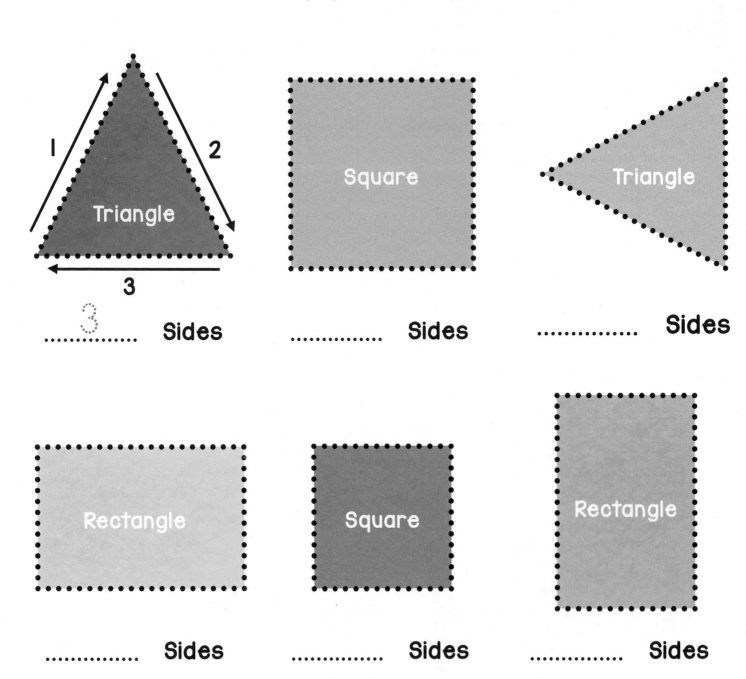

.... Sides

.... Sides

.... Sides

.... Sides

.... Sides

.... Sides

Fun with Shapes

Trace each Shape. Find a Shape in each picture and draw a line to match it to the one you traced.

Join the dots and color to create a beautiful veil.

Join the dots and color to bring to life a cute elephant.

Fun with Patterns

Observe the pattern and draw the shape that comes next. Color the shape accordingly.

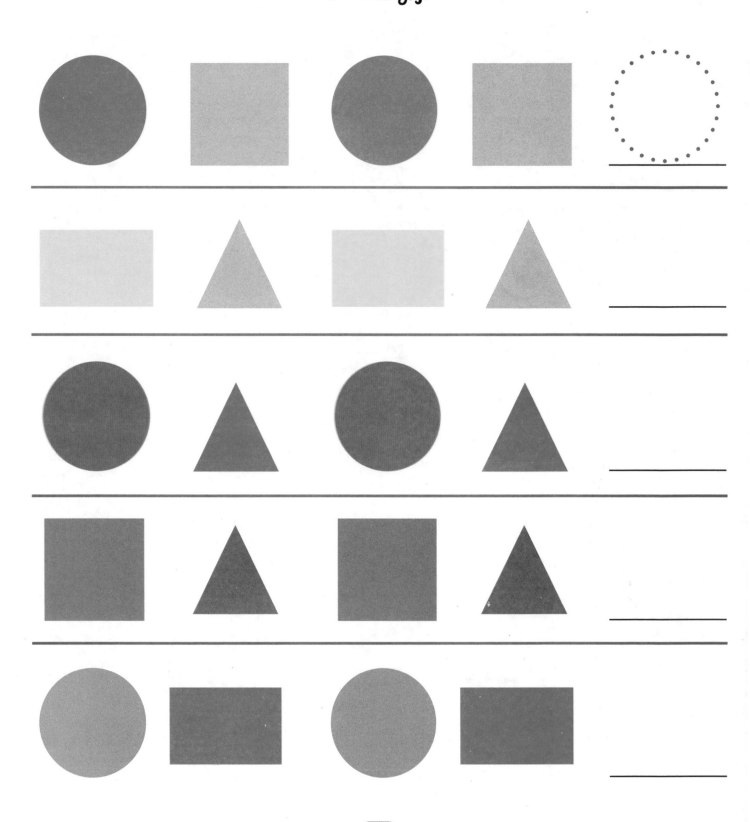

Same but Different

Find and circle the odd one out.

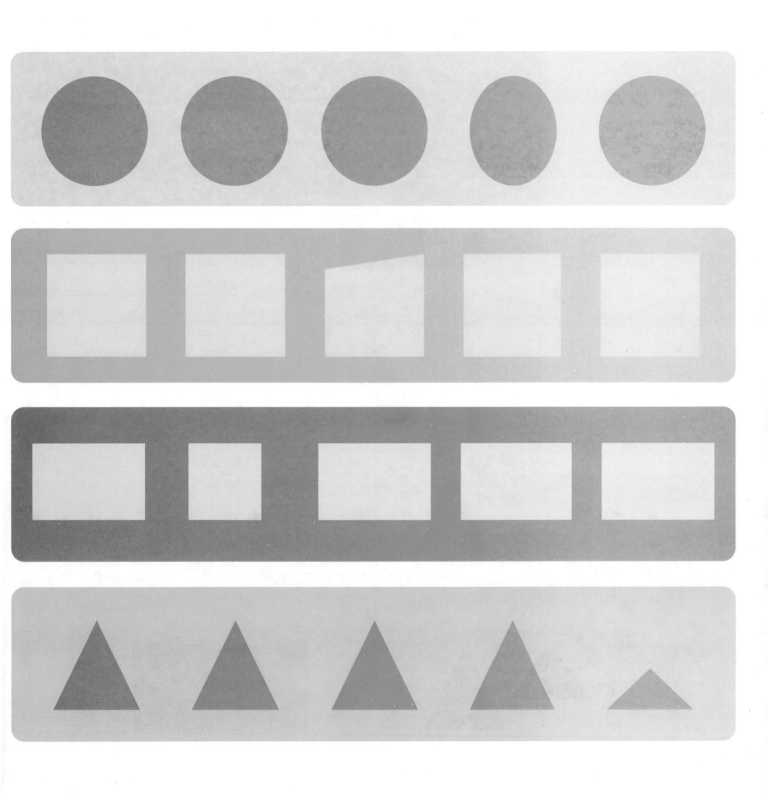

Matching Shapes

Count the number of each shape in the rocket below. Pick the box of shapes that you think is right to create another such rocket.

Matching Shapes

Count the number of each shape in the engine below. Pick the box of shapes that you think is right to create another such rocket.

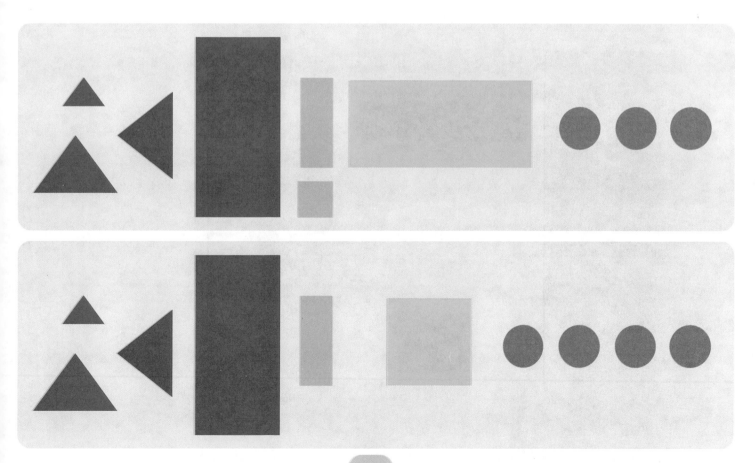

Tracing Fun

Complete the given shapes by drawing the remaining half part.
Fill in the matching color.

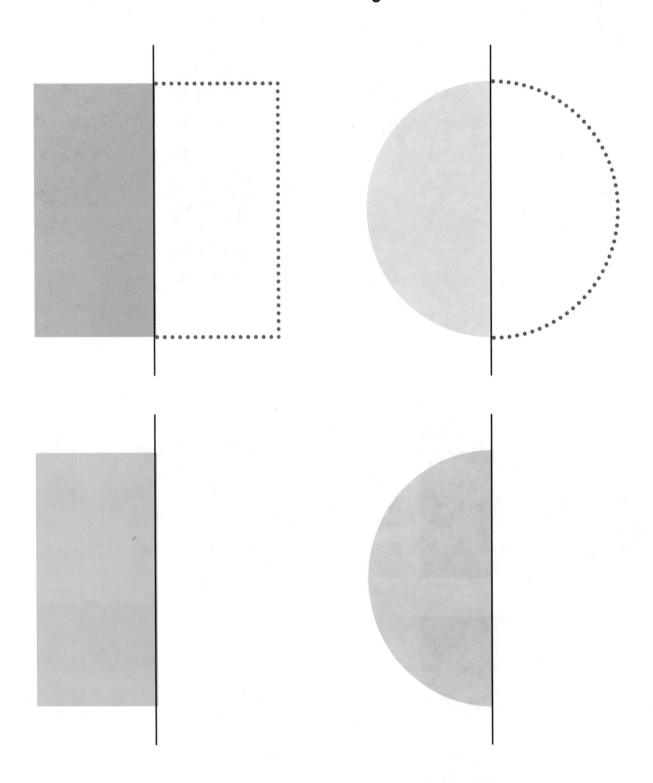

Tracing Fun

Complete the given Shapes by drawing the remaining half.
Fill in the matching color.

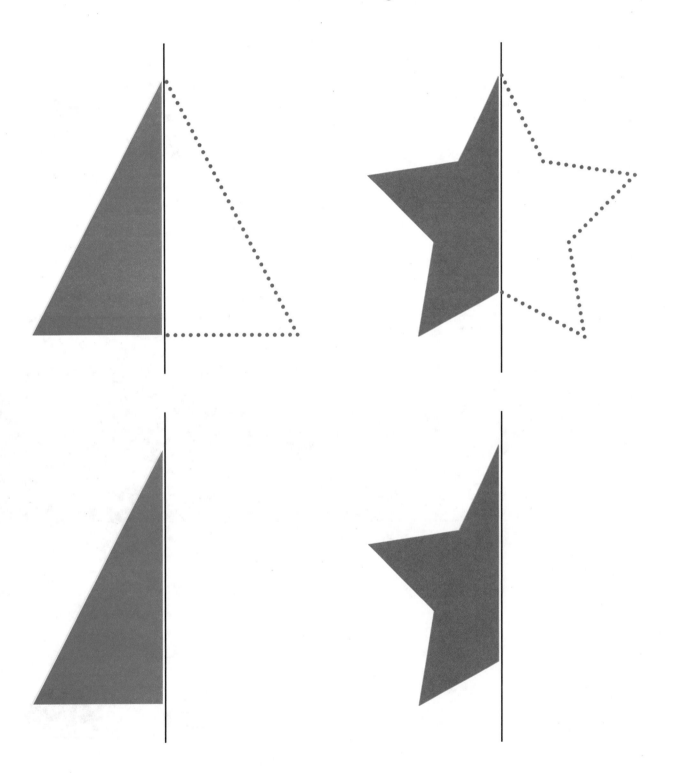

Let's Find Out

Observe and find the object that does not match with the shape given on the left.

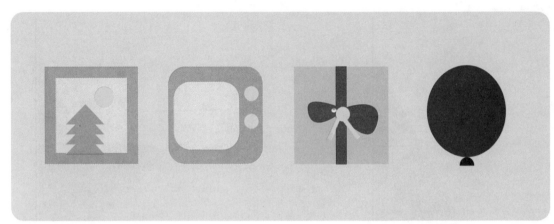

Fun with Shadows

Match the pictures with their shadows on the right.

How do you know your shapes?

Color the shapes accordingly.

Circle ➡ Red   Diamond ➡ Green

Rectangle ➡ Blue   Hexagon ➡ Orange

Square ➡ Yellow   Triangle ➡ Purple

How many Sides?

Trace and count the sides of each shapes and circle the correct number.

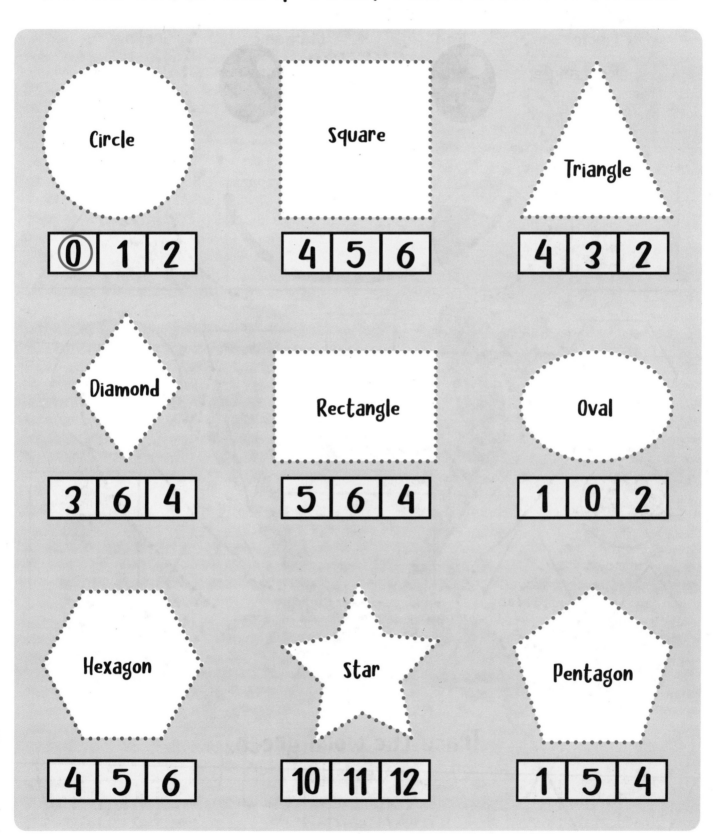

Circle   ⓪ 1 2

Square   4 5 6

Triangle   4 3 2

Diamond   3 6 4

Rectangle   5 6 4

Oval   1 0 2

Hexagon   4 5 6

Star   10 11 12

Pentagon   1 5 4

Trace the dots and experiment with shades of green!

Trace the word green.

GREEN   GREEN   GREEN

Circle all the green things.

Trace the dots and experiment with shades of blue!

Trace the word blue.

Circle all the blue things.

Trace the dots and experiment with shades of red!

Trace the word red.

RED   RED   RED

Circle all the red things.

Trace the dots and experiment with shades of yellow!

Trace the word yellow.

YELLOW YELLOW YELLOW

Circle all the yellow things.

Trace the dots and experiment with shades of purple!

Trace the word purple.

PURPLE PURPLE PURPLE

Circle all the purple things.

Trace the dots and experiment with shades of pink!

Trace the word pink.

PINK   PINK   PINK

Circle all the pink things.

Trace the dots and experiment with shades of orange!

Trace the word orange.

ORANGE   ORANGE

Circle all the orange things.

Trace the dots and experiment with shades of brown!

Trace the word brown.

BROWN   BROWN

Circle all the brown things.

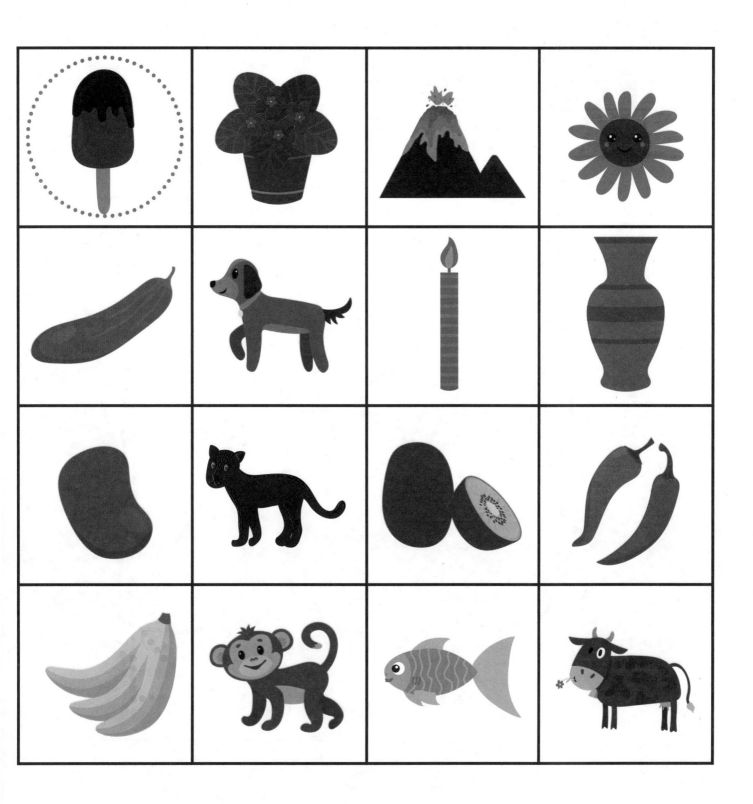

Trace the dots and experiment with shades of black!

Trace the word black.

BLACK BLACK BLACK

Circle all the black things.

Matching Colors

Identify the colors of these fruits and animals by matching them against the colors given on the right.

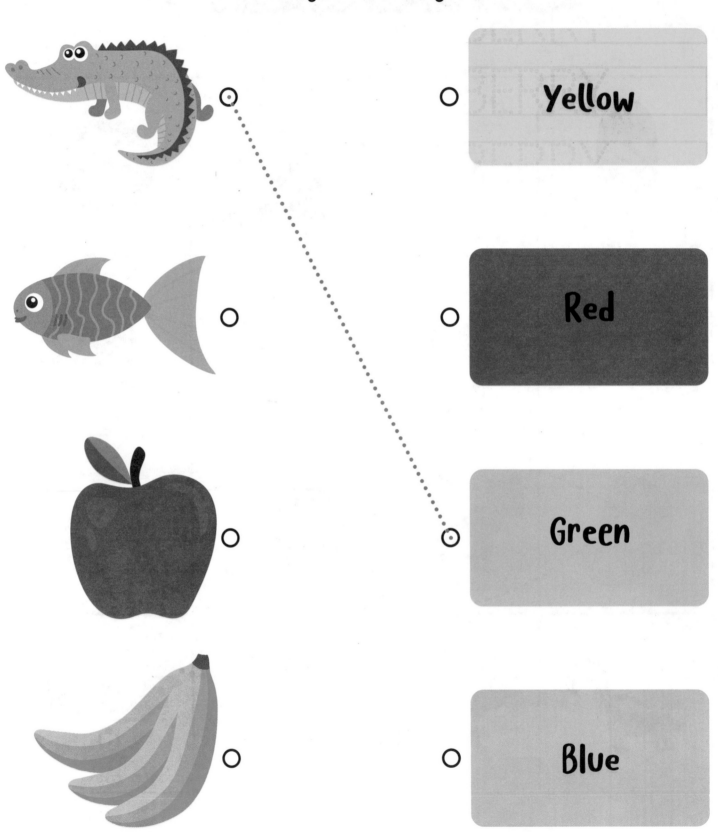

Yellow

Red

Green

Blue

Matching Colors

Identify the colors of these fruits and animals by matching them against the colors given on the right.

Pink

Brown

Black

Purple

Orange

Color the picture and write the names of the colors that you use.

color: ....

Color the picture and write the names of the colors that you use.

color: ....

Color all the red things.

Circle all the yellow things.

Color all the blue things.

Circle all the orange things.

Color all the green things.

Circle all the purple things.

Color all the pink things.

Circle all the brown things.

Identify the fruit and trace its name. Join the dots to draw and then color the fruit.

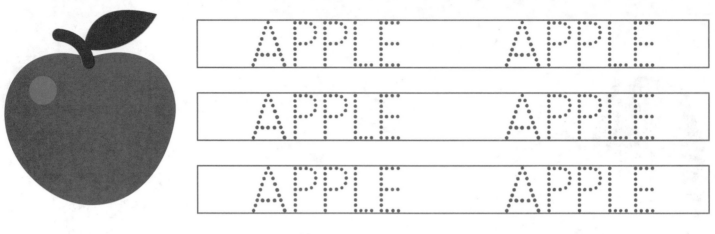

APPLE   APPLE
APPLE   APPLE
APPLE   APPLE

Identify the fruit and trace its name. Join the dots to draw and then color the fruit.

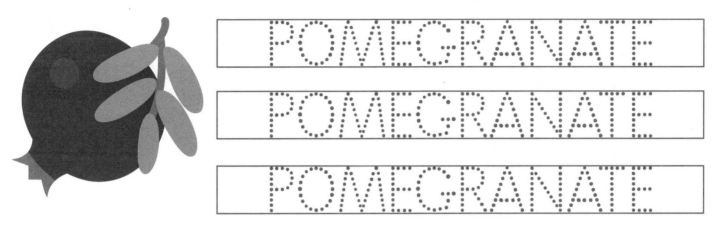

POMEGRANATE

POMEGRANATE

POMEGRANATE

Identify the fruit and trace its name. Join the dots to draw and then color the fruit.

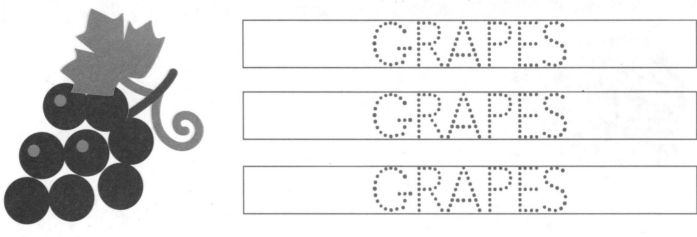

GRAPES

GRAPES

GRAPES

Identify the fruit and trace its name. Join the dots to draw and then color the fruit.

BLACKBERRY

BLACKBERRY

BLACKBERRY

Identify the fruit and trace its name. Join the dots to draw and then color the fruit.

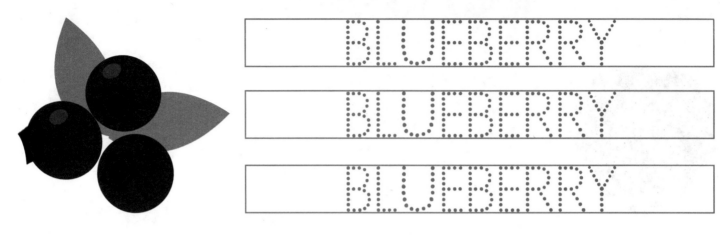

BLUEBERRY

BLUEBERRY

BLUEBERRY

Identify the fruit and trace its name. Join the dots to draw and then color the fruit.

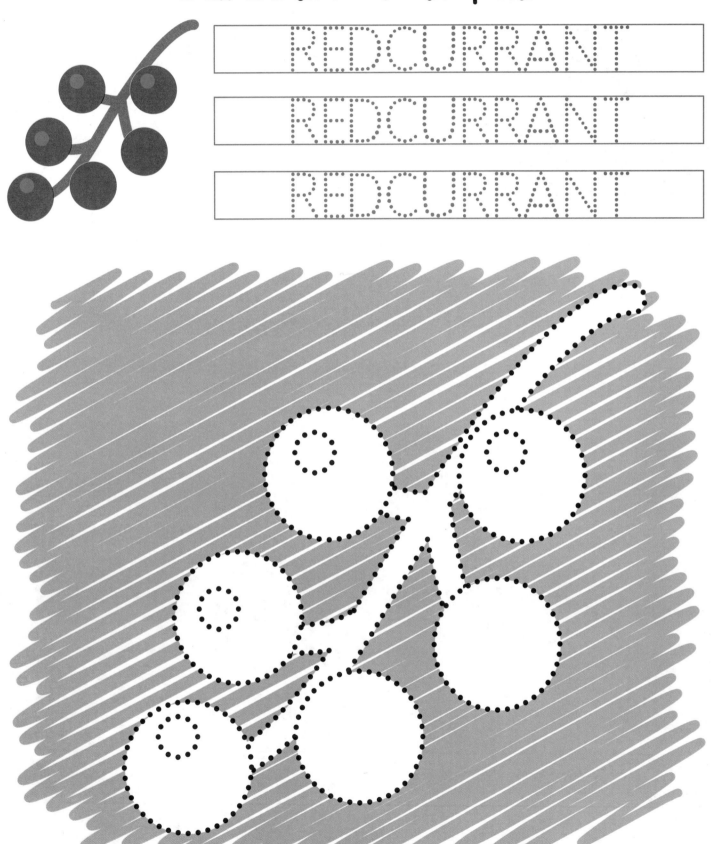

REDCURRANT

REDCURRANT

REDCURRANT

Identify the fruit and trace its name. Join the dots to draw and then color the fruit.

CHERRY

CHERRY

CHERRY

Identify the fruit and trace its name. Join the dots to draw and then color the fruit.

PEACH   PEACH

PEACH   PEACH

PEACH   PEACH

Identify the fruit and trace its name. Join the dots to draw and then color the fruit.

PLUM   PLUM

PLUM   PLUM

PLUM   PLUM

Identify the fruit and trace its name. Join the dots to draw and then color the fruit.

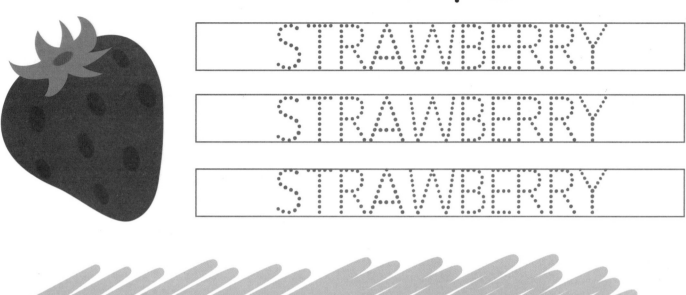

STRAWBERRY

STRAWBERRY

STRAWBERRY

Identify the fruit and trace its name. Join the dots to draw and then color the fruit.

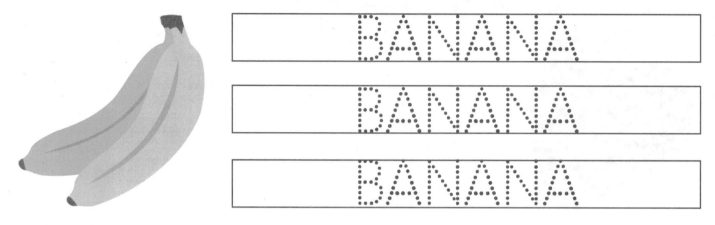

BANANA

BANANA

BANANA

Identify the fruit and trace its name. Join the dots to draw and then color the fruit.

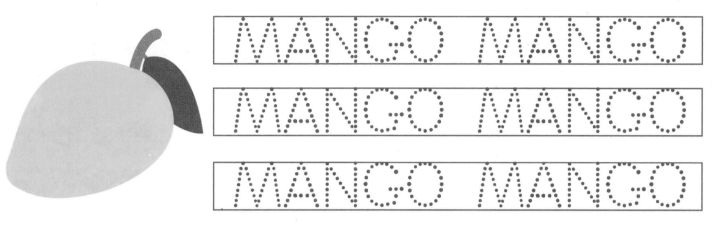

MANGO MANGO

MANGO MANGO

MANGO MANGO

Complete these fruits by matching their two halves.

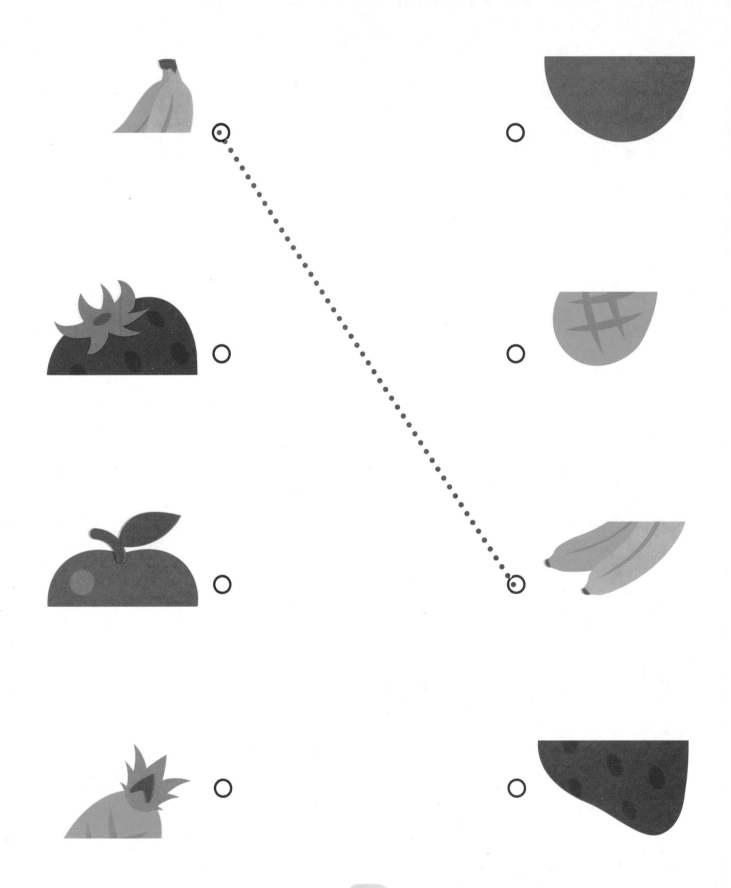

Complete these fruits by matching their two halves.

Count the times each fruit appears in the picture and write the number in the box.

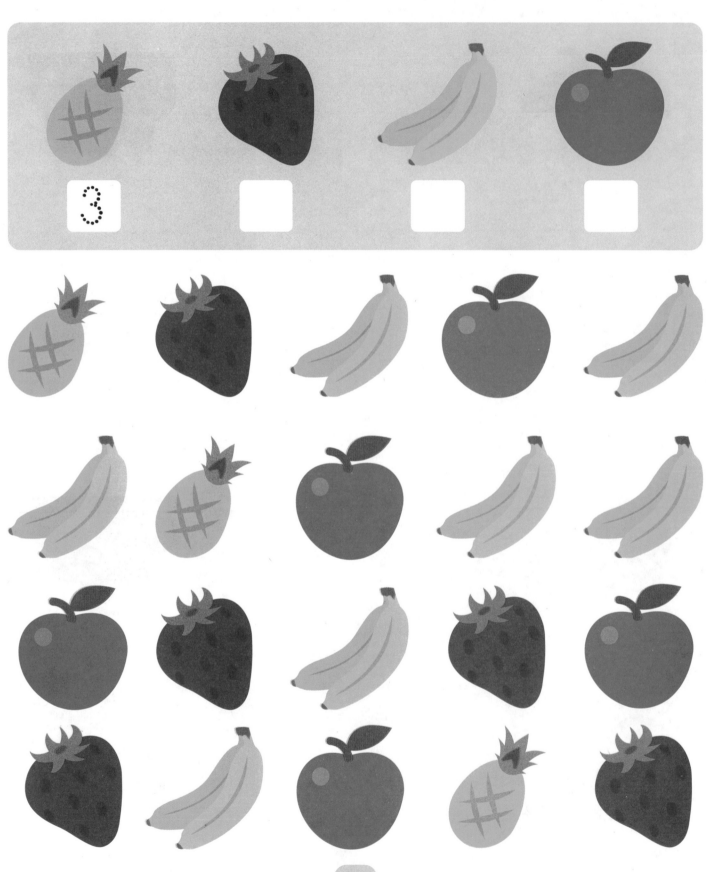

Count the times each fruit appears in the picture and write the number in the box.

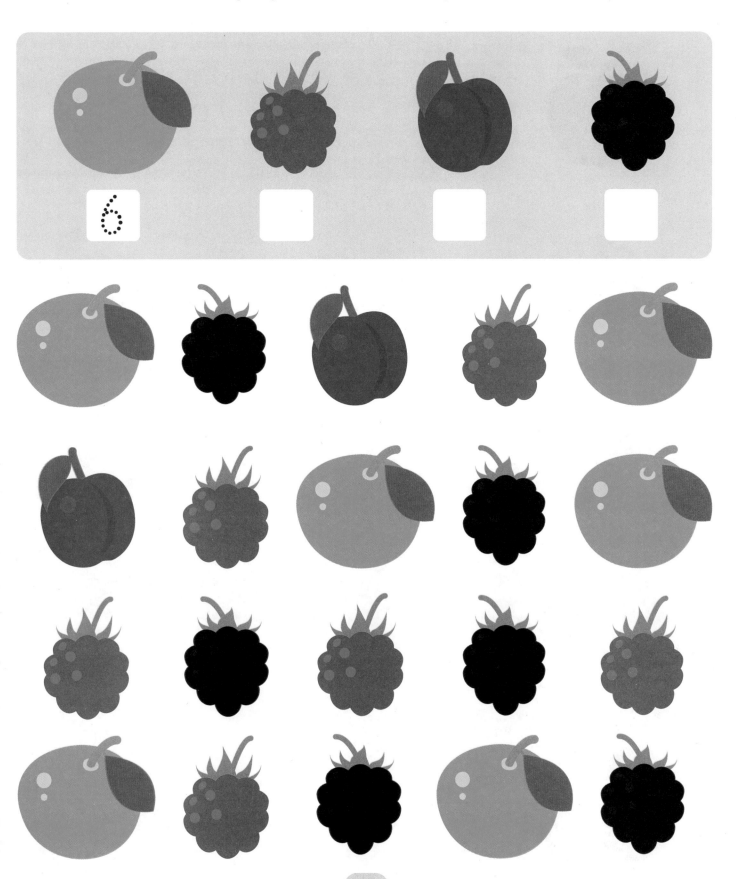

Match these fruits with their shadows.

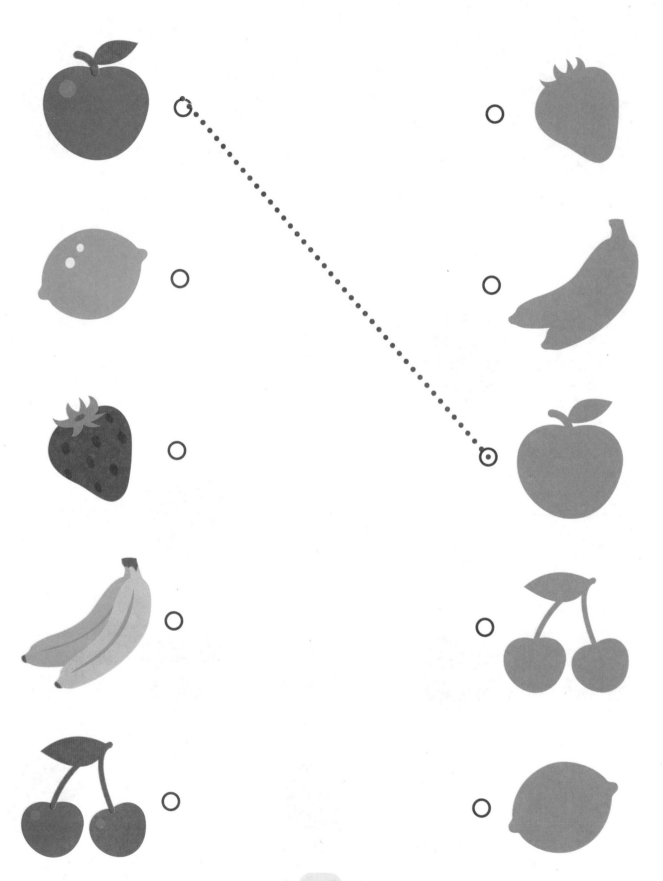

Match these fruits with their shadows.

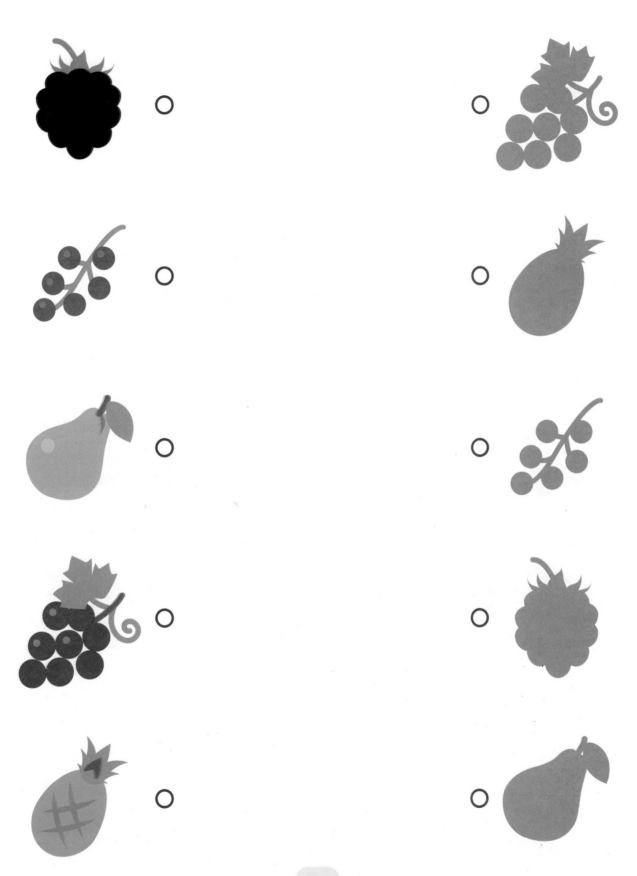

Identify the fruits and solve the crossword puzzle.

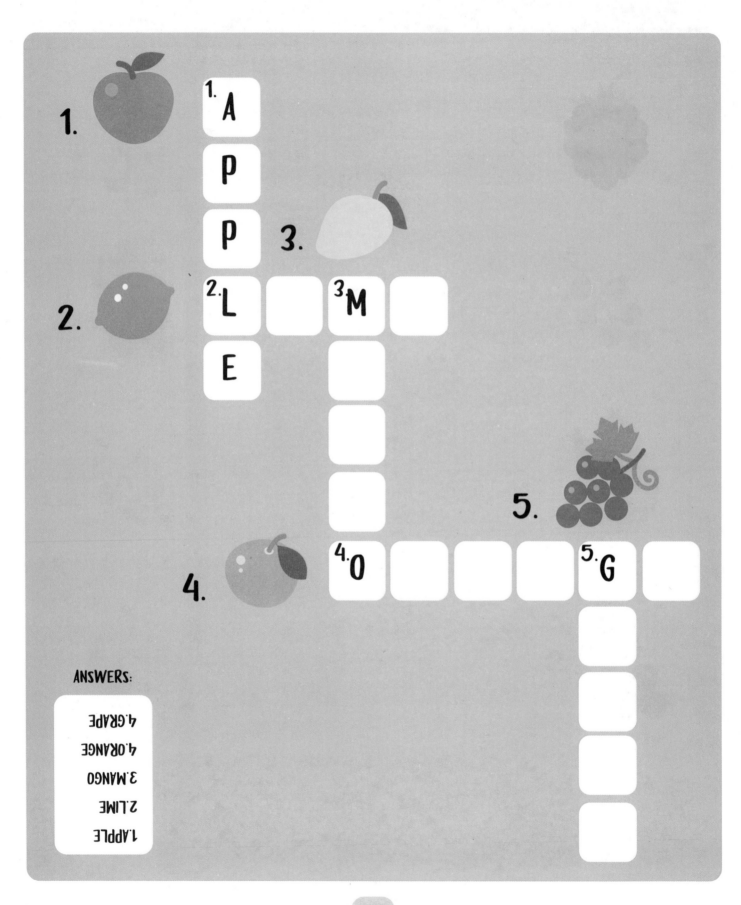

1.

^{1.}A
P
P
^{2.}L
E

2.

3.

³M

5.

^{4.}O ___ ___ ___ ^{5.}G ___

4.

ANSWERS:

1.APPLE
2.LIME
3.MANGO
4.ORANGE
4.GRAPE

Identify the fruits and solve the crossword puzzle.

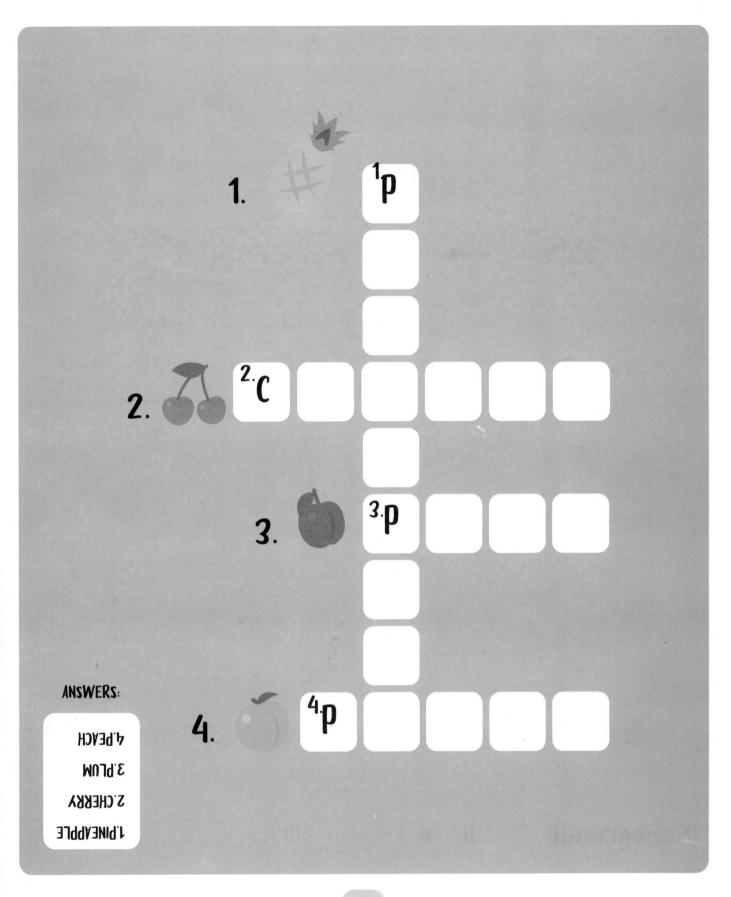

1. ¹P

2. ²C

3. ³P

4. ⁴P

ANSWERS:
1.PINEAPPLE
2.CHERRY
3.PLUM
4.PEACH

Identify the fruits and write the missing letter in the names given below. Trace the path and match the fruit with its name.

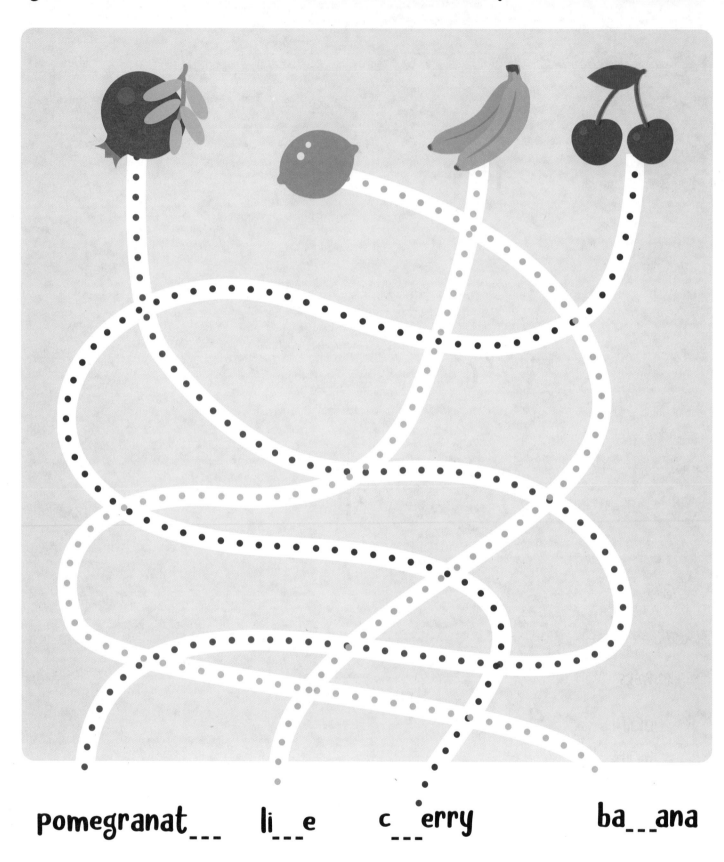

pomegranat___   li___e   c___erry   ba___ana

Identify the fruits and write the missing letter in the names given below. Trace the path and match the fruit with its name.

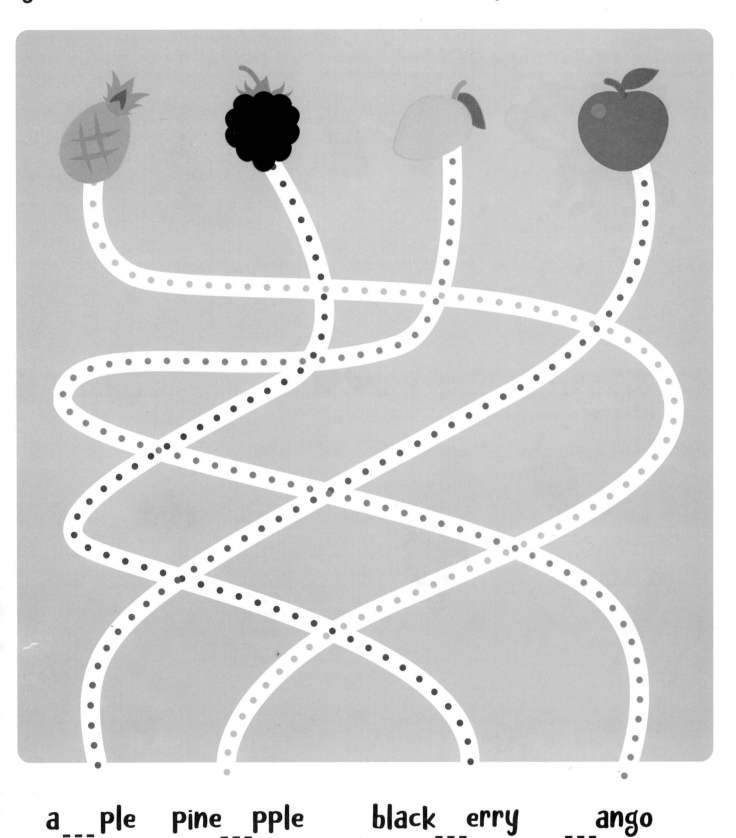

a___ple   pine___pple   black___erry   ___ango

Help the monkey collect only fruits on this page.

Help dino collect only fruits on this page.

Identify the animal and match it with its name.

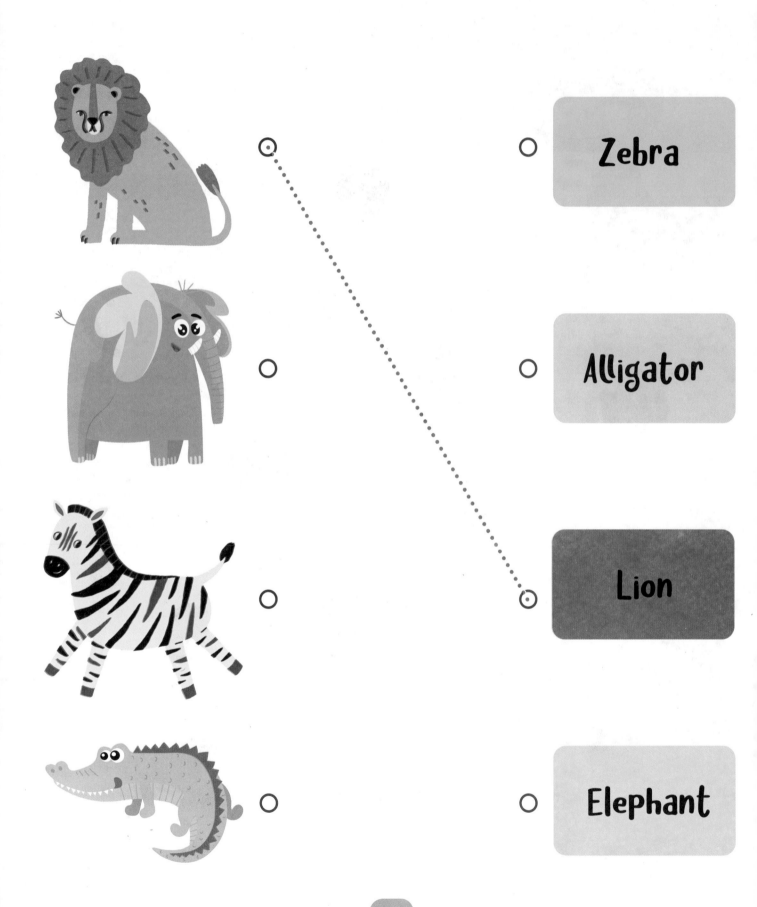

Zebra

Alligator

Lion

Elephant

Identify the animal and match it with its name.

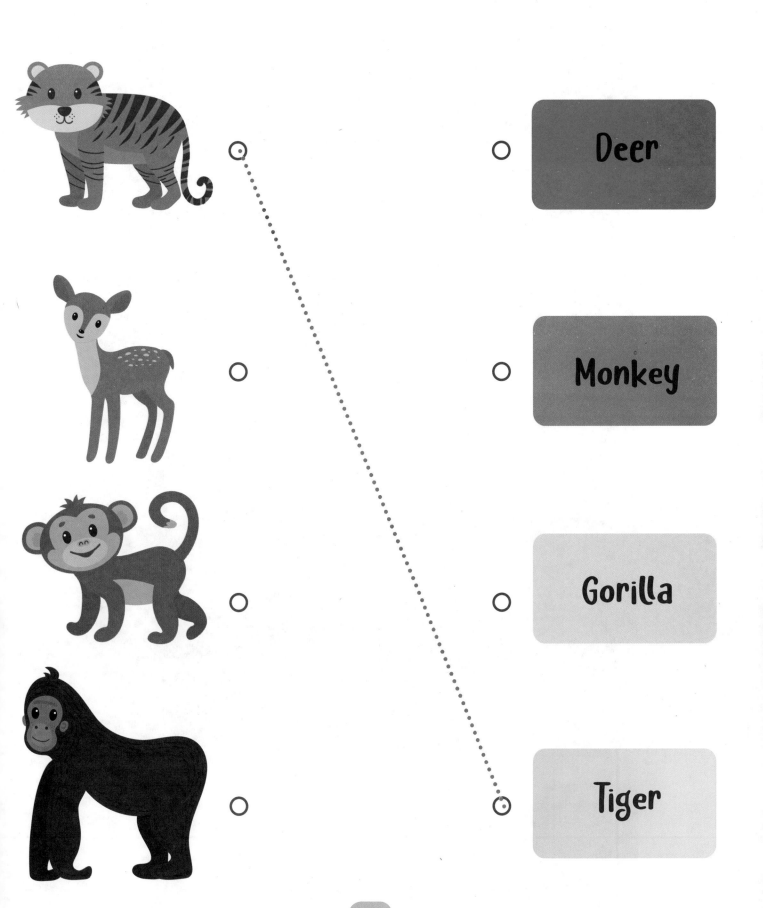

Deer

Monkey

Gorilla

Tiger

Find 7 Differences ⭕

Find 6 Differences⭕

Help the little deer find his dad by tracing the path.

Help this monkey find some bananas by tracing the path.

Complete the animals by matching their two halves.

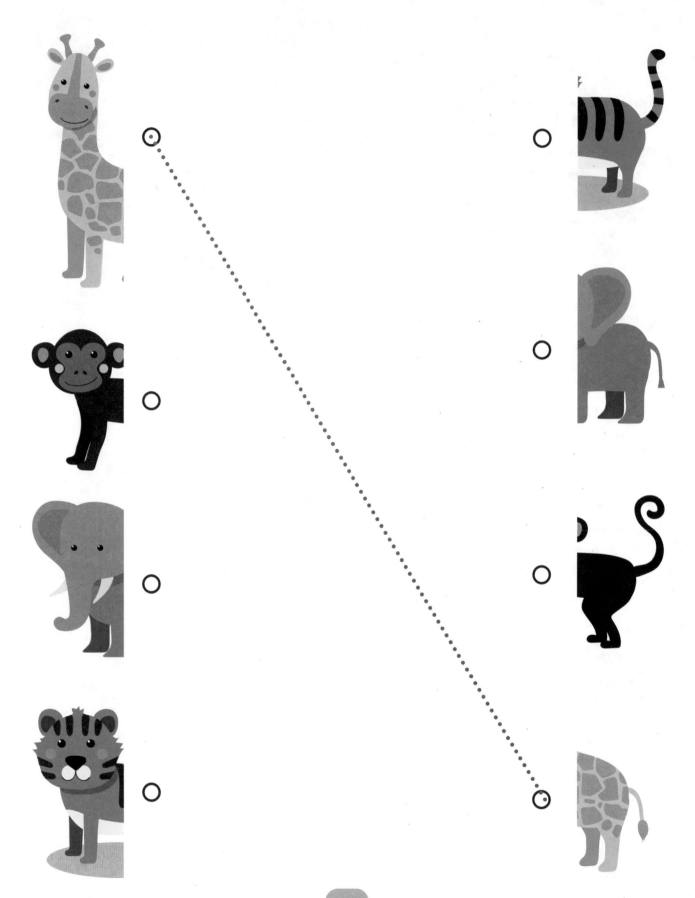

Complete the animals by matching their two halves.

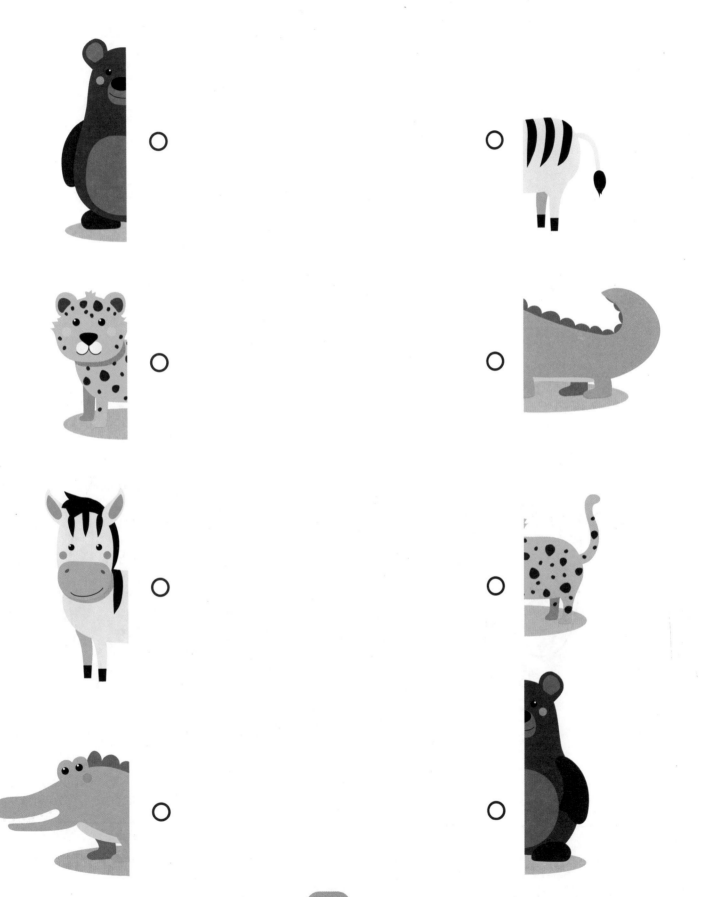

Dot to Dot
Join the dots and color the picture.

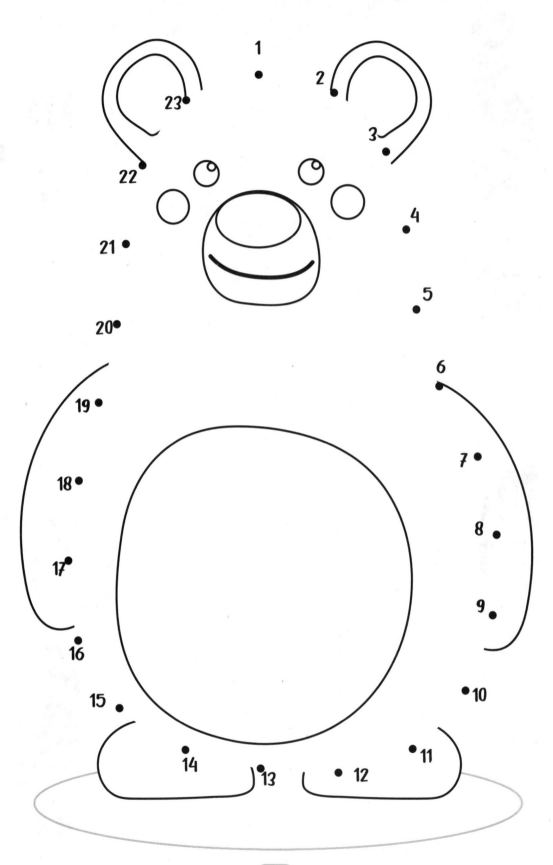

Dot to Dot
Join the dots and color the picture.

Match the animals with their shadows.

Match the animals with their shadows.

Identify the animals and write their names to solve the crossword puzzle.

2. I

3.

1. M O ⬜ ⬜ E ⬜

⬜

4. R ⬜ ⬜ ⬜ O

Identify the animals and write their names to solve the crossword puzzle.

3. G

1. E

2. E ☐ ☐ A

E

4. T ☐ ☐ ☐ R

ANSWERS:
1. elephant
2. zebra
3. giraffe
4. tiger

Match these animals and patterns.

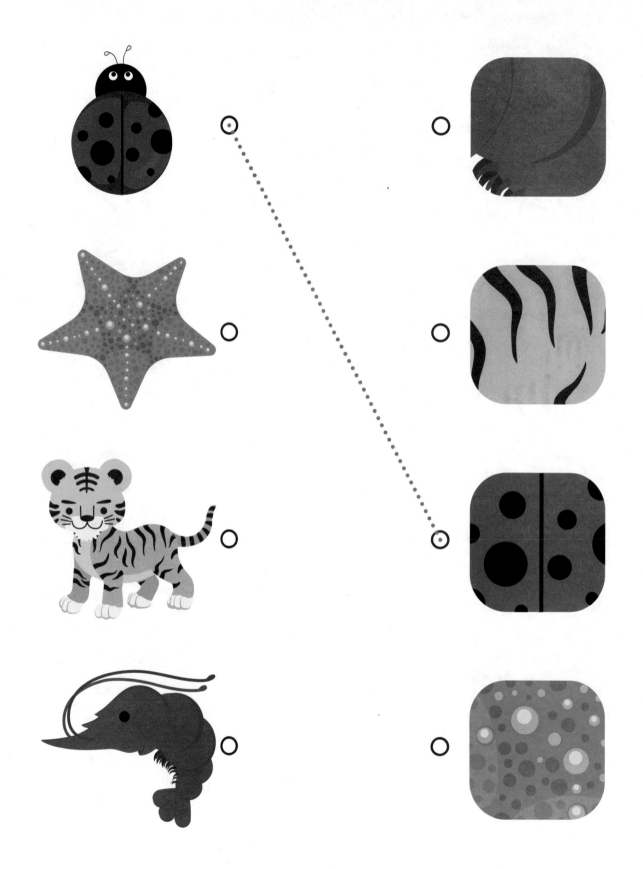

Match these animals and patterns.

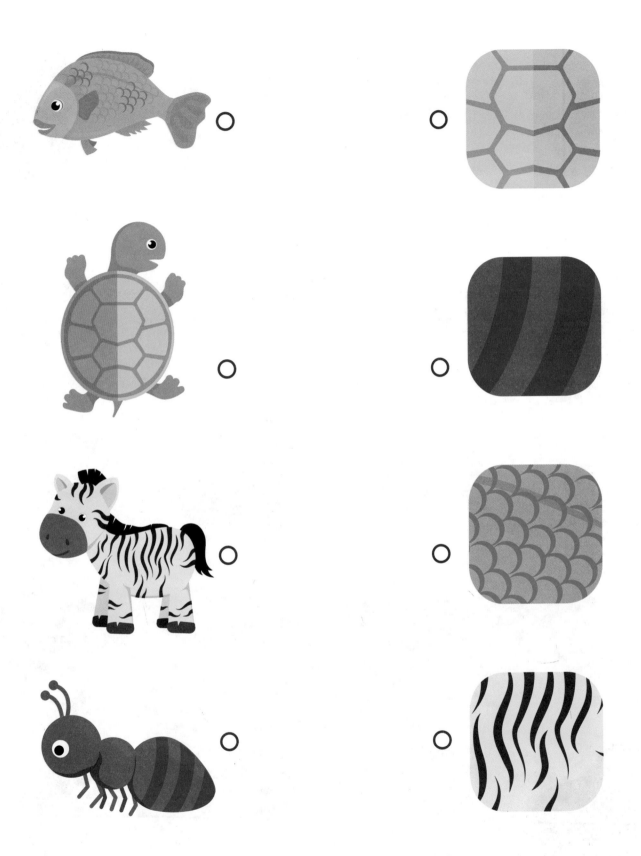

Count the times each animal can be found in the picture and write the number in the box.

Count the times each animal can be found in the picture and write the number in the box.

Identify the animal and color the picture. Use the given letters to trace its name in the box below.

N L I O

L I O N

Identify the animal and color the picture. Use the given letters to trace its name in the box below.

G I T E R

T I G E R

Identify the animal and color the picture. Use the given letters to trace its name in the box below.

E   Y   M   O   N   K

M O N K E Y

Identify the animal and color the picture. Use the given letters to trace its name in the box below.

I R G O L L A

GORILLA

Identify the marine animal and match it with its name.

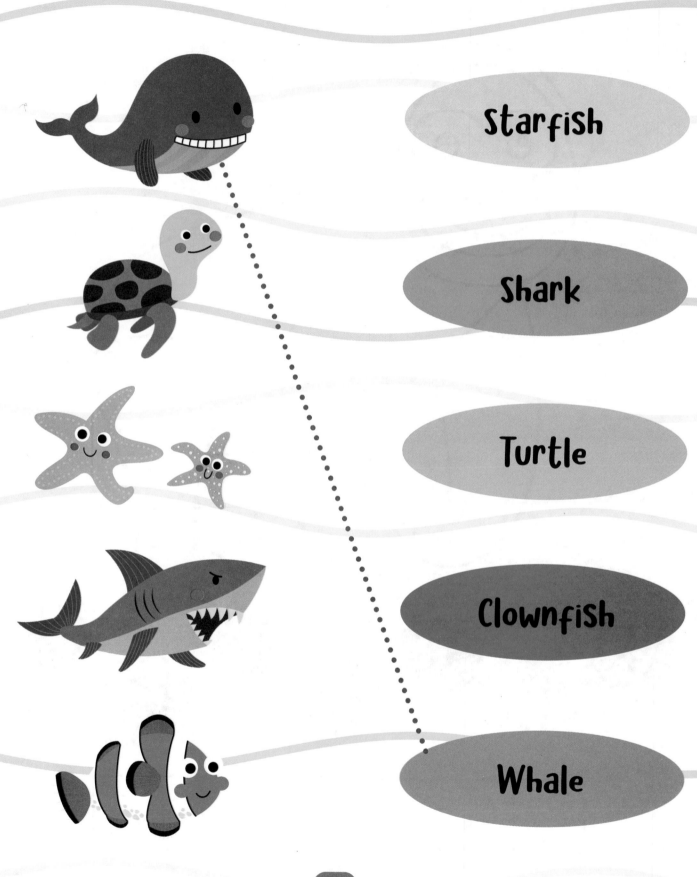

Starfish

Shark

Turtle

Clownfish

Whale

Identify the marine animal and match it with its name.

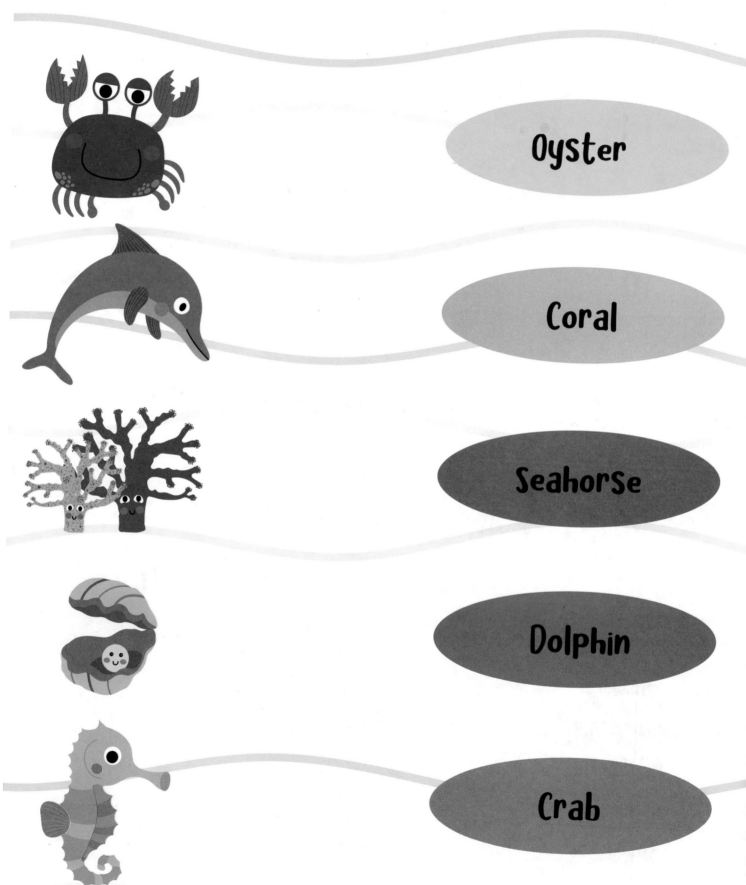

Oyster

Coral

Seahorse

Dolphin

Crab

Identify the marine animals and write their names to solve the crossword puzzle.

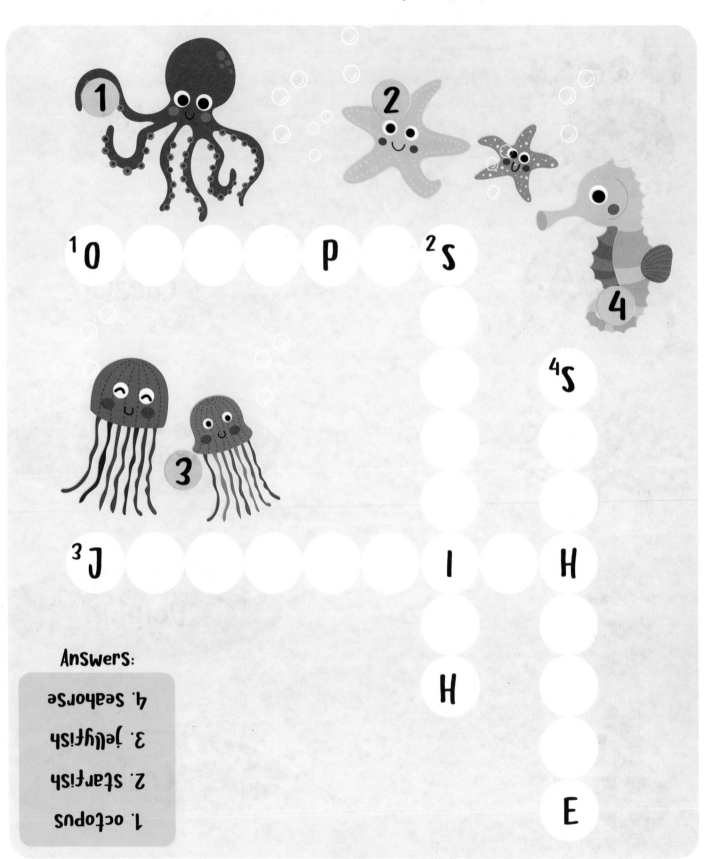

^{1}O ○ ○ ○ P ○ ^{2}S

^{4}S

^{3}J ○ ○ ○ ○ ○ I H

H

E

Identify the marine animals and write their names to solve the crossword puzzle.

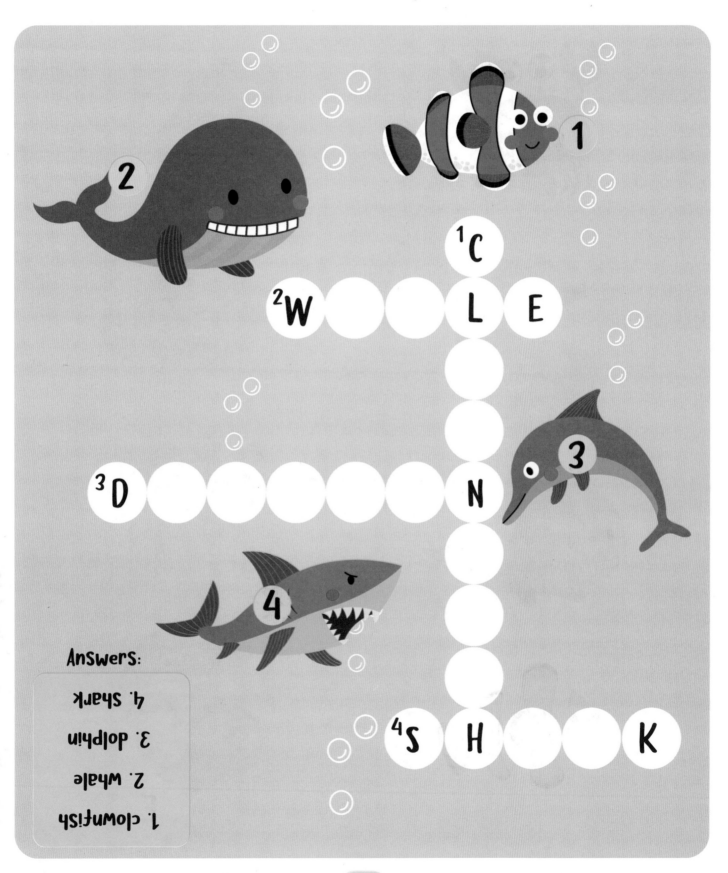

Answers:

1. clownfish
2. whale
3. dolphin
4. shark

Match the marine animals with their Shadows.

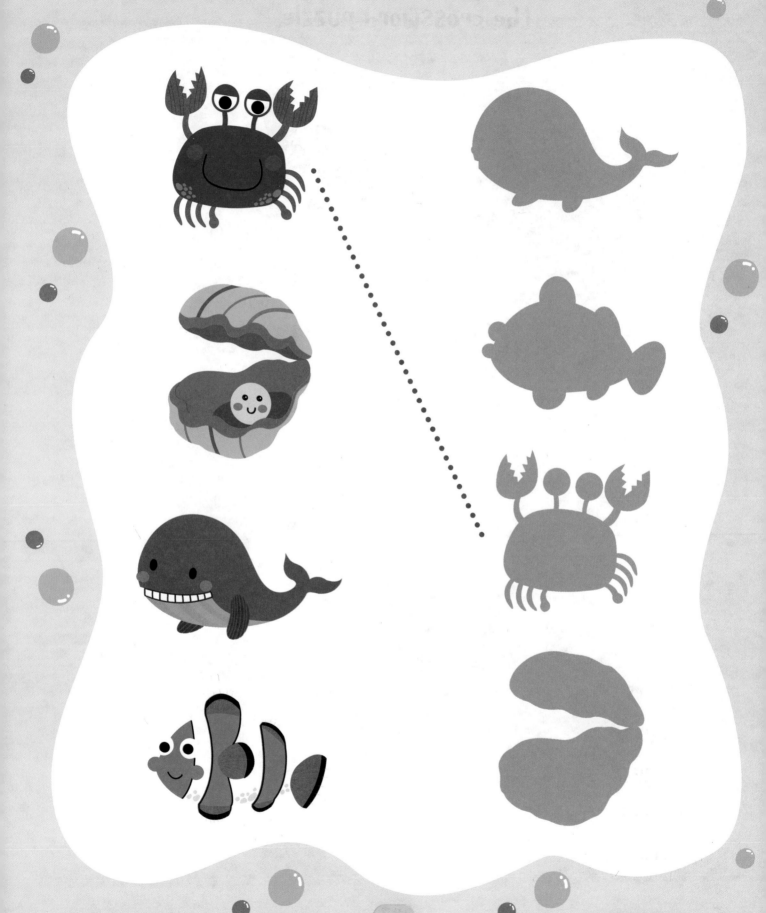

Match the marine animals with their shadows.

Help the jellyfish meet her mom.

The Matching Game

Match the boxes with the same number of marine animals.

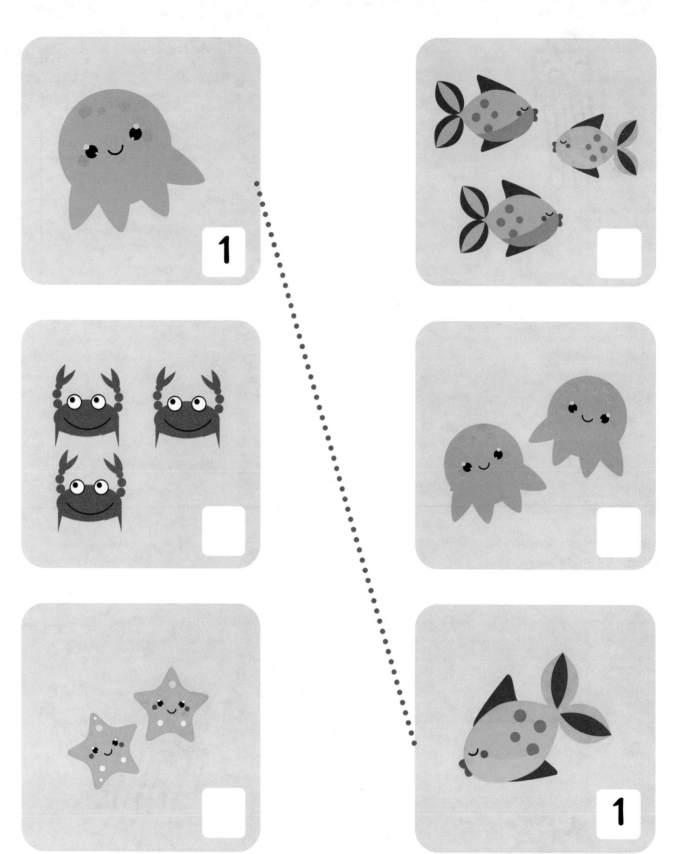

The Matching Game
Match the boxes with the same number of marine animals.

Find the Differences
Find and circle 5 differences between these the pictures.

Find the Differences
Find and circle 5 differences between these the pictures.

How many are going to the left, how many to the right?

Left   right

How many are going to the left, how many to the right?

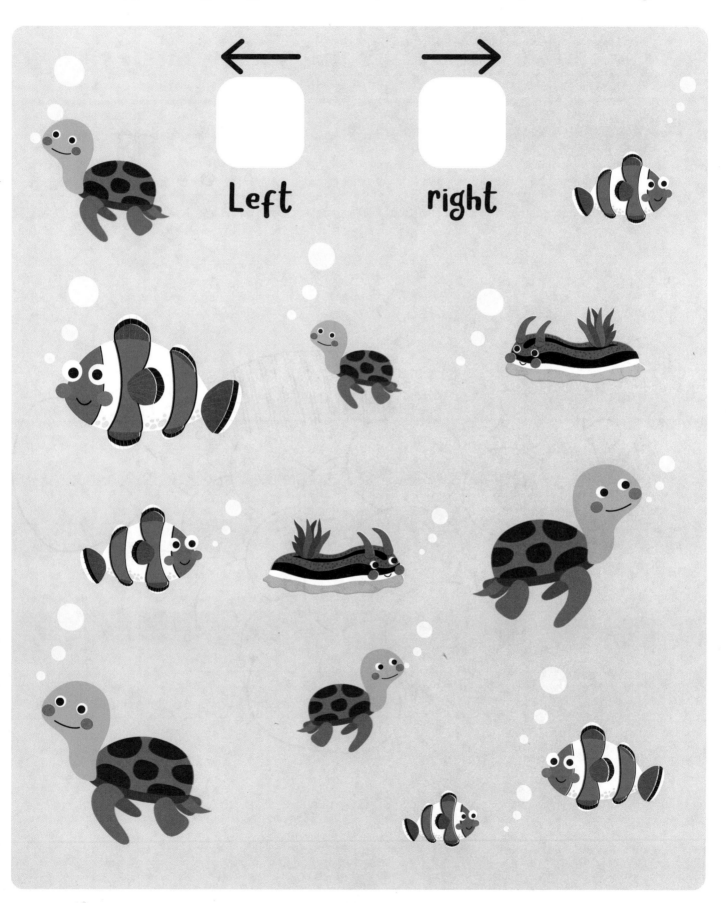

← Left   → right

Connect the Dots

Connect the Dots

Trace the dots and color the picture!

Trace the dots and color the picture!

Let's Look Closer!

Observe the images and circle the odd one out.

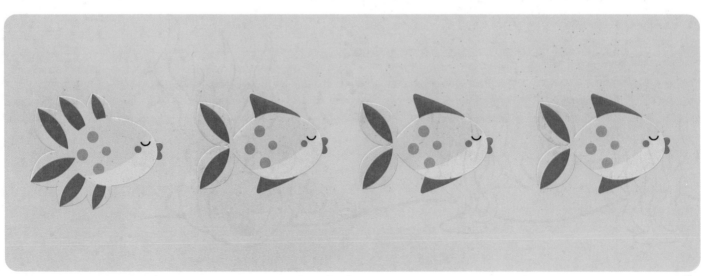

Let's Look Closer!

Observe the images and circle the odd one out.

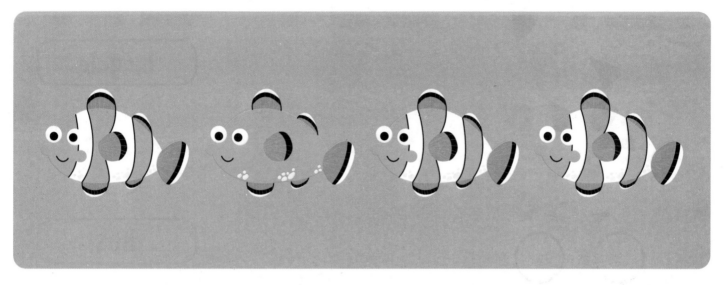

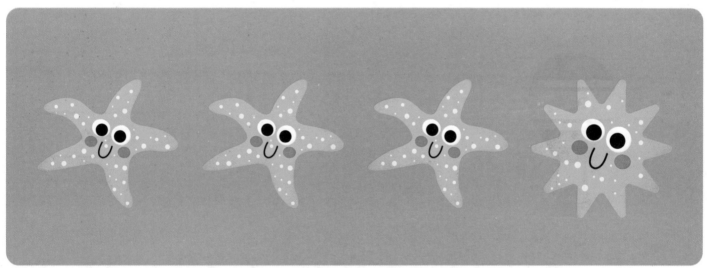

Identify the mode of transport and match it with its name given in the box.

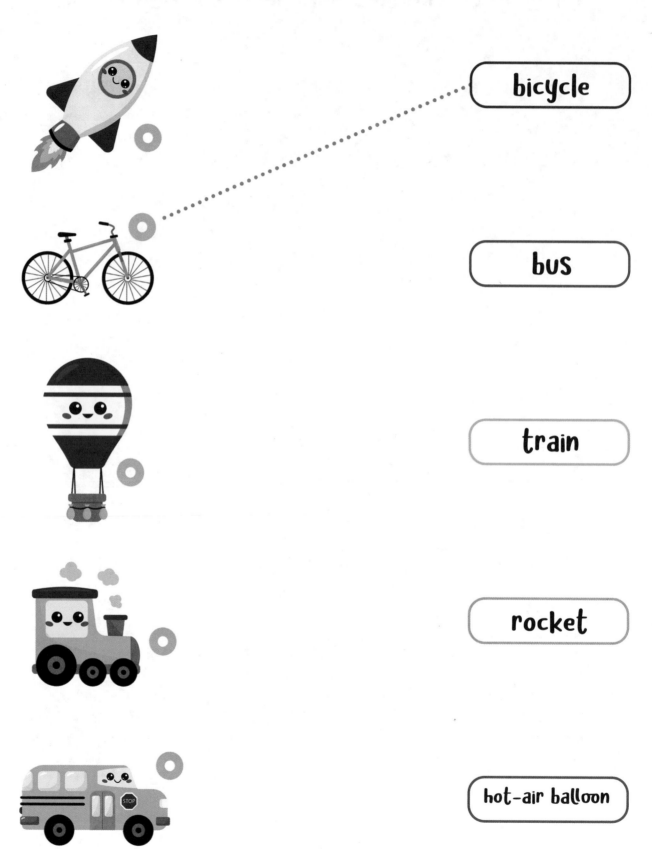

bicycle

bus

train

rocket

hot-air balloon

Identify the mode of transport and match it with its name given in the box.

helicopter

airplane

truck

car

Ship

Where do they move?

Identify the mode of transport and match it with where it moves.

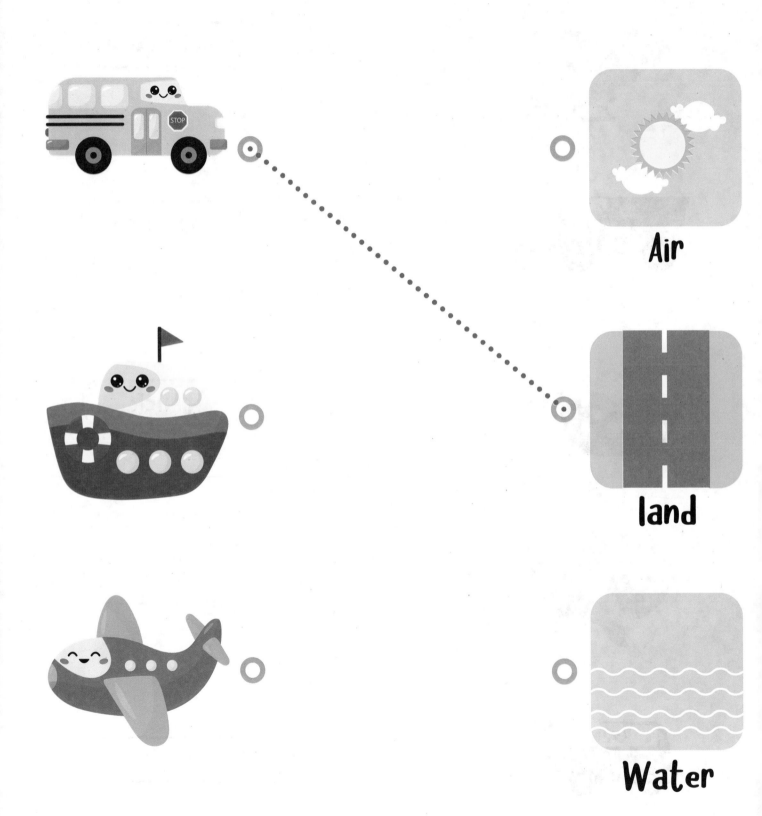

Air

land

Water

Where do they move?

Identify the mode of transport and match it with where it moves.

 ○

 ○

 ○

○

Air

○

land

○

Water

Join the dots and color the bus.

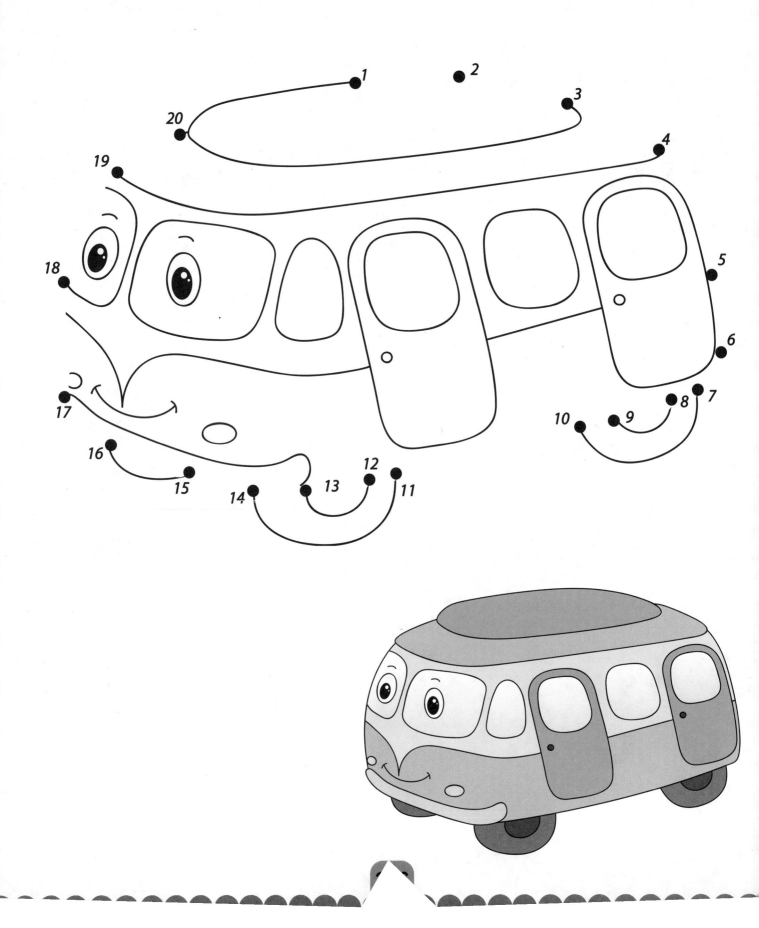

Join the dots and color the truck.

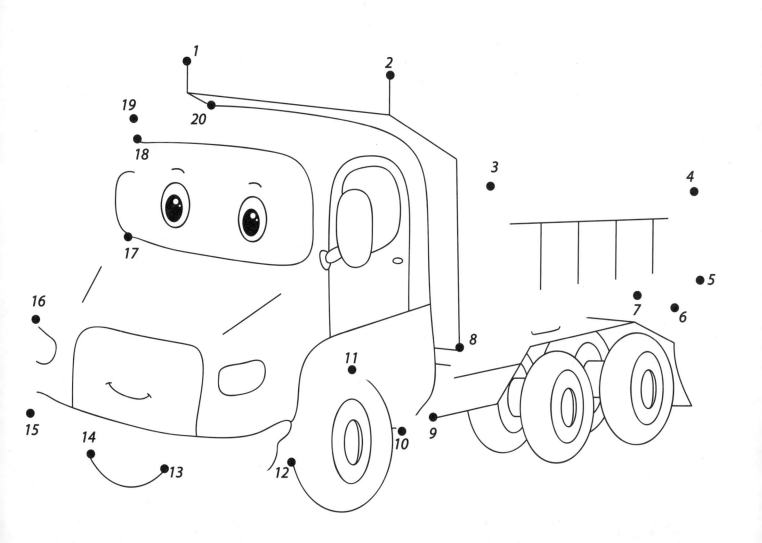

Match these vehicles with their shadows.

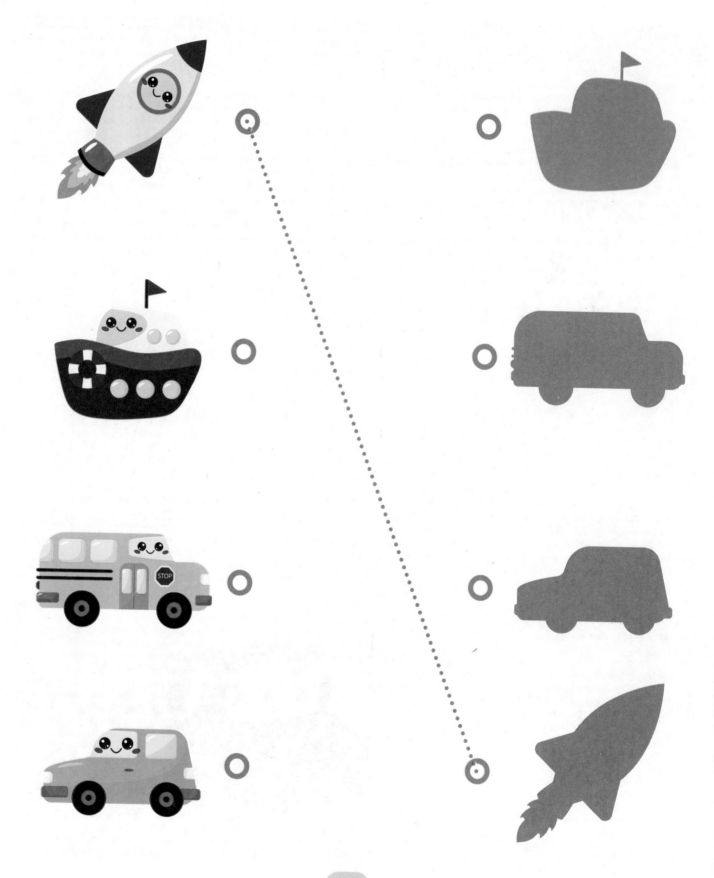

Match these vehicles with their shadows.

Identify the vehicle and Solve the crossword puzzle.

1.

2.

2. H

1. A _ _ _ L _ _ E

3. T _ _ _ K

4. C _ R

3.

4.

Identify the vehicle and solve the crossword puzzle.

2. H

1. T | A | N

2.

1.

4. S

3. B I P L E

P

3.

4.

N

Color me!

Policeman

Color me!

Fireman

Color Me!

Doctor

Color Me!

Artist

Help these community leaders find their modes of transport by matching them correctly.

Fireman

Concrete mixer

Policeman

Ambulance

Doctor

Police car

Builder

Fire engine

Help these community leaders find their modes of transport by matching them correctly.

○ Carpenter

○

Hair dryer

○ Hairdresser

○

Snorkelling mask

○ Archaeologist

○

Drilling machine

○ Diver

○

Geological tool

Count the times each object appears in the picture and write the number in the box.

7

Count the times each object appears in the picture and write the number in the box.

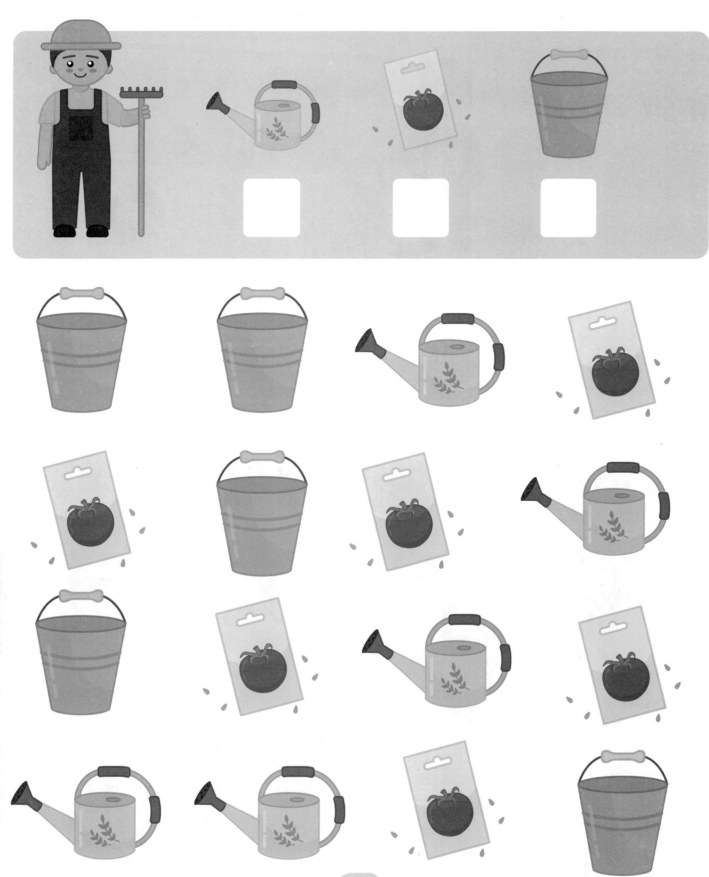

Identify the community helpers and write their names to solve the crossword puzzle.

¹P
²D O [ ] [ ] [ ] R
O
A
G A [ ] [ ] [ ] [ ] [ ] [ ] [ ] [ ]
⁴F
R
N
N

Answer:

1.postman
2.doctor
3.gardener
4.fireman

Identify the community helpers and write their names to solve the crossword puzzle.

Across and down grid:

1. P
2. M _ _ D
3. B
4. A R _ _ _ T
N

Answer:
1. policeman
2. maid
3. builder
4. artist

Match these modes of transport with their shadows.

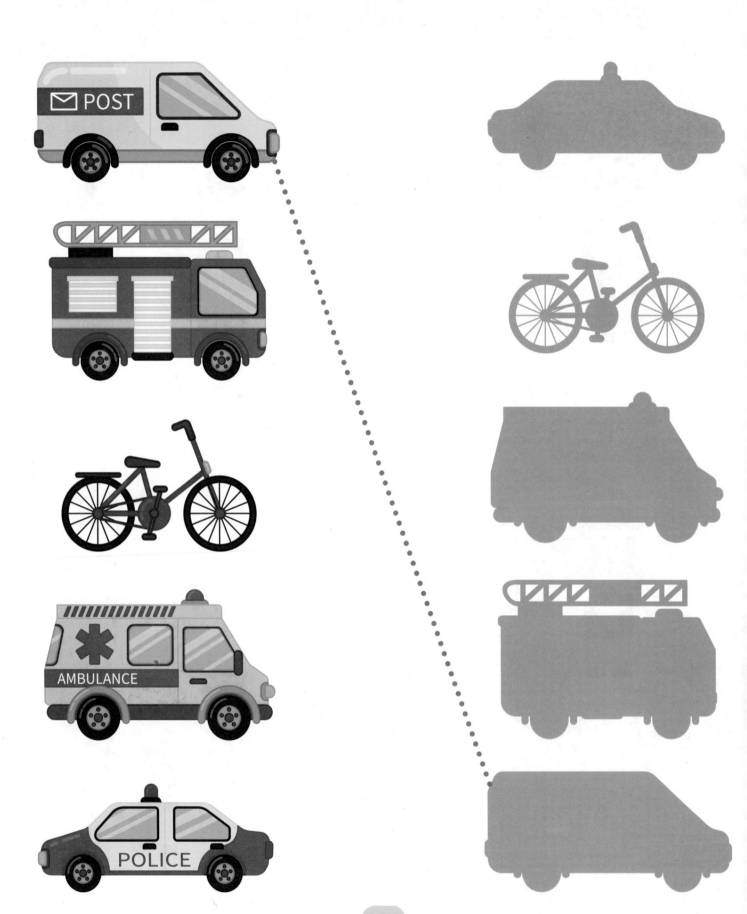

Match these tools with their shadows.

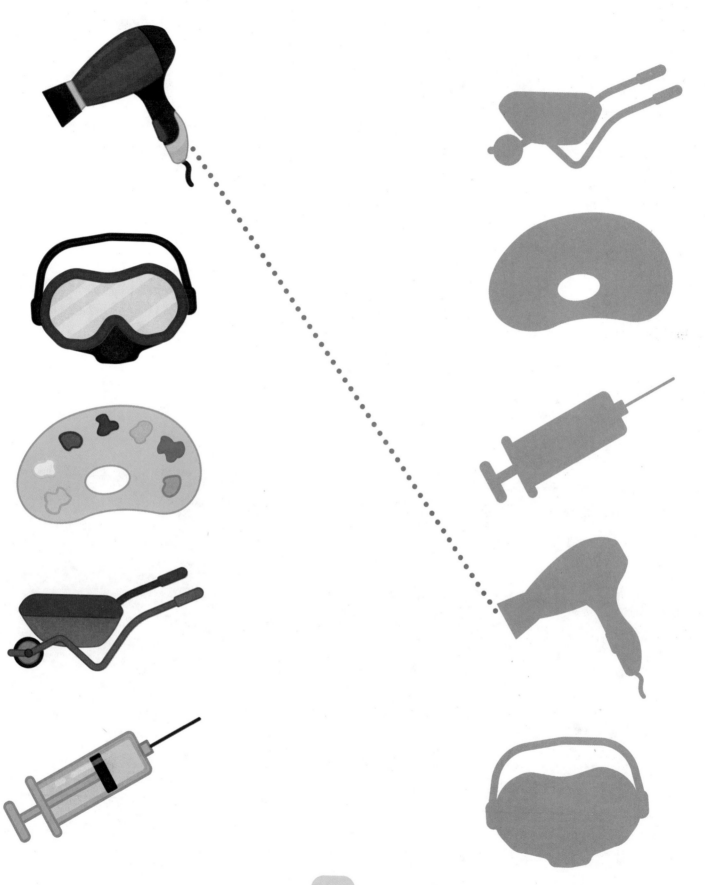

Help the doctor reach her bag while collecting all the medicines.

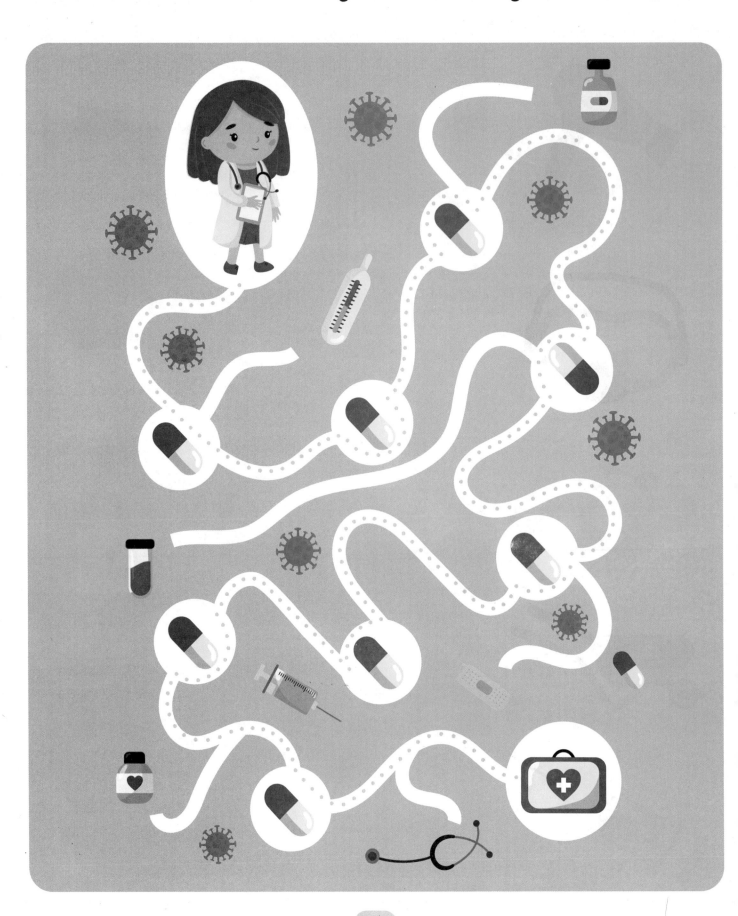

Help the fireman reach his firetruck by following the right pipe.

Circle the objects used by firefighters.

Circle the objects used by policeman.

Circle the objects used by carpenters.

Circle the objects used by a hairdresser.

Circle the correct objects for doctor.

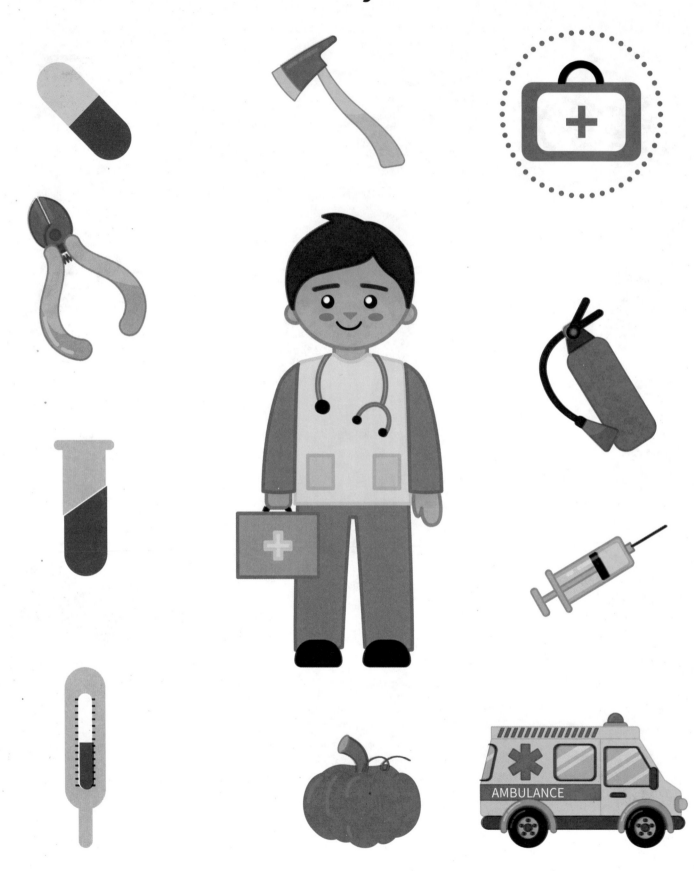

Circle the correct objects for gardener.

Identify the sense given on the left and match it against the right use of it.

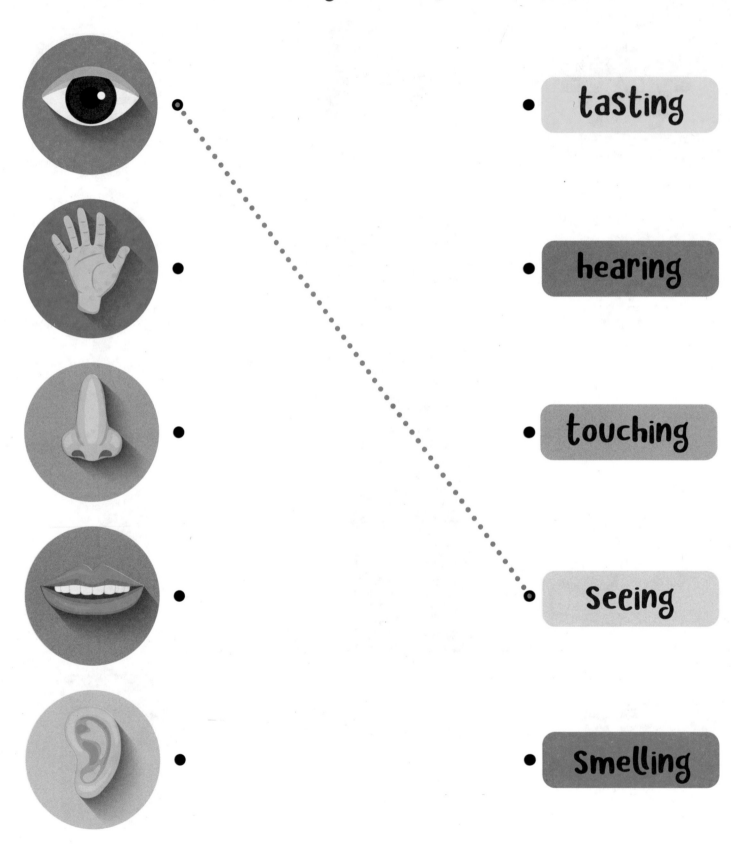

tasting

hearing

touching

seeing

smelling

Talking Sense

Fill in the blank by identifying the sense.

The boy is .... at the bug.

looking   touching   smelling

Talking Sense

fill in the blank by identifying the sense.

The girl is .... a cat.

hearing   touching   tasting

Talking Sense

fill in the blank by identifying the sense.

The girl is .... a flower.

Smelling   touching   tasting

Talking Sense

fill in the blank by identifying the sense.

The boy is .... an ice cream.

touching   tasting   smelling

Talking Sense

fill in the blank by identifying the sense.

The boy is .... to the radio.

Smelling   listening   tasting

Circle all the objects related to the Sense of Sight.

Circle all the objects related to the sense of hearing.

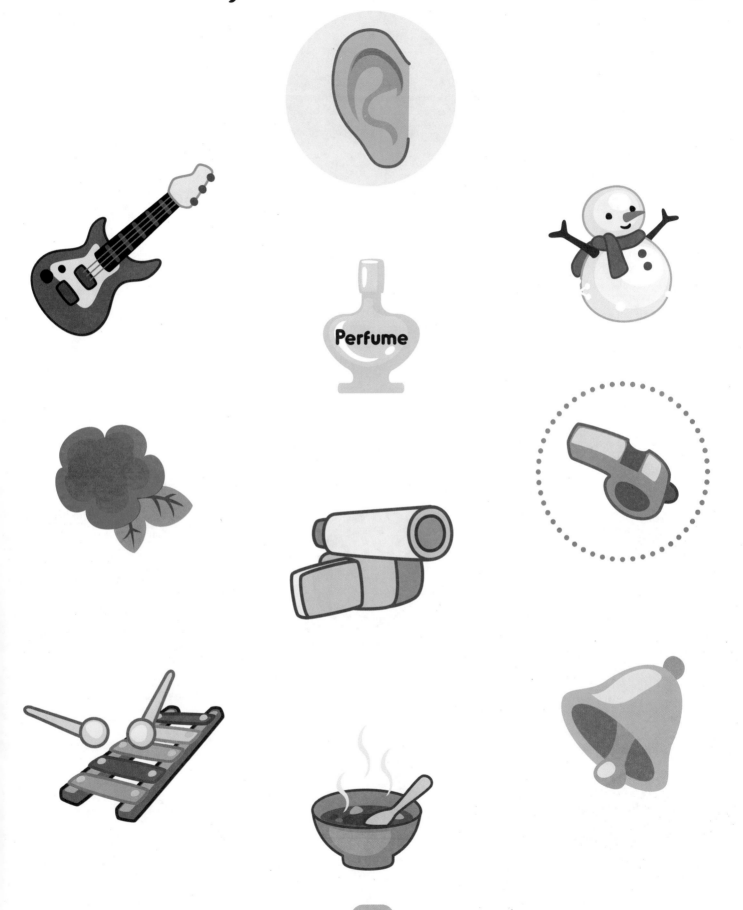

Perfume

Circle all the objects related to the sense of taste.

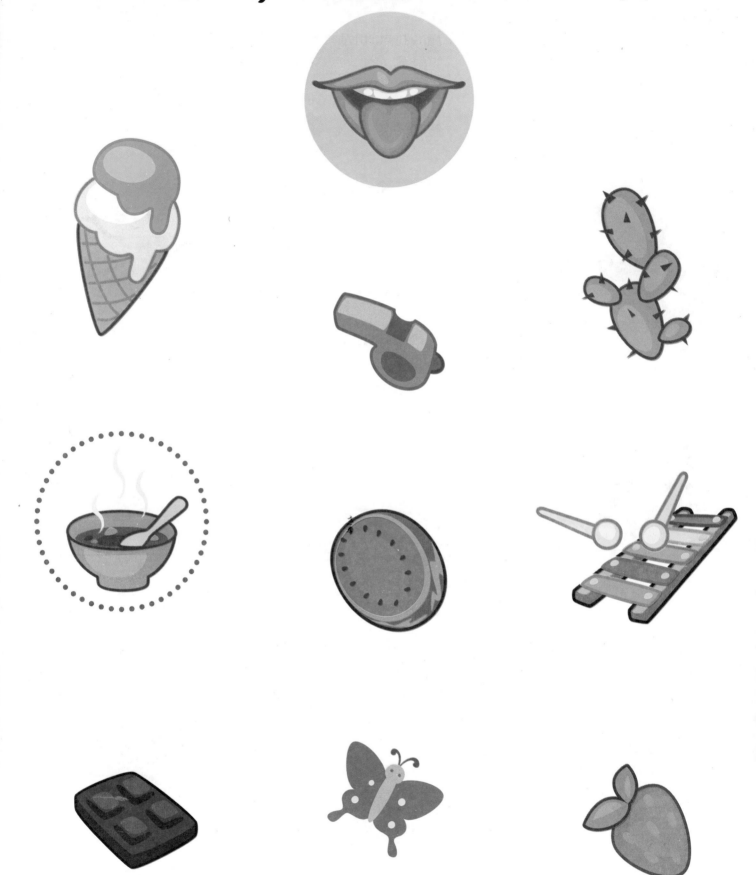

Circle all the objects related to the Sense of Smell.

Circle all the objects related to the sense of touch.

Identify the senses on the left and match them to their uses on the right.

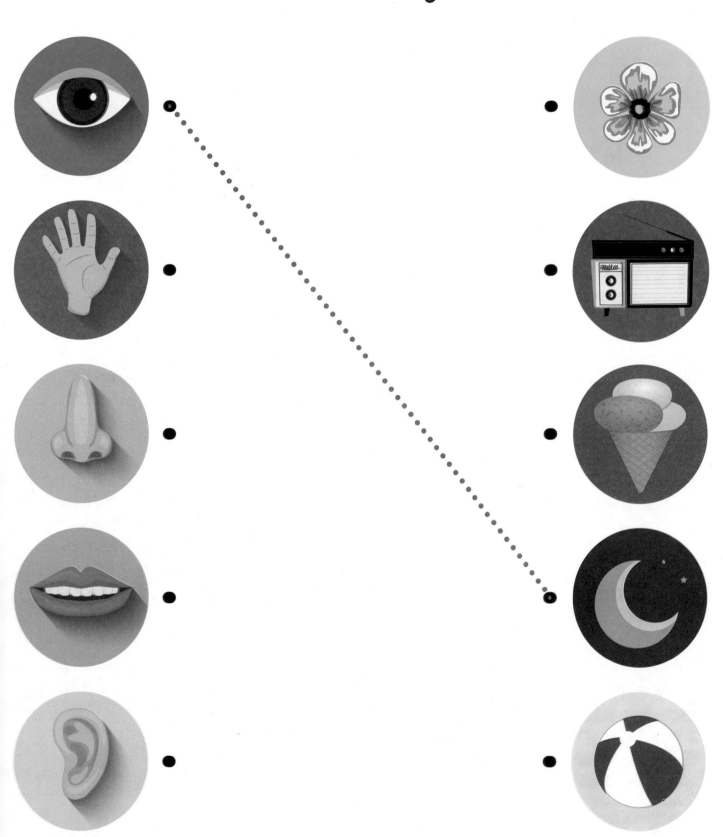

Match the Opposites

day

many

one

frown

Smile

fast

slow

night

Match the Opposites

summer

short

empty

cold

hot

winter

long

full

Circle the biggest one.

Circle the biggest one.

Circle the smallest one.

Circle the smallest one.

Odd One Out!

Circle the object that is different from the rest.

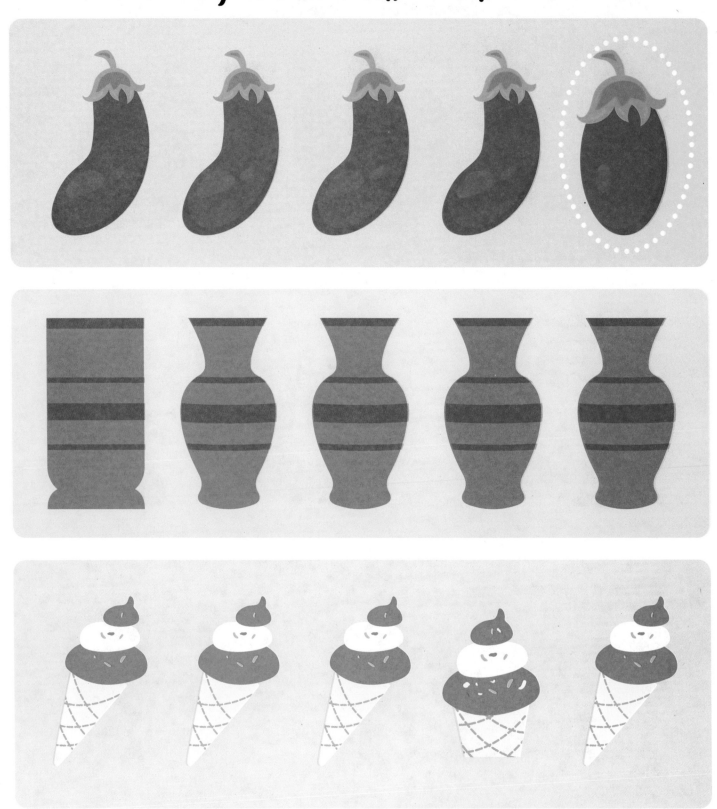

Odd One Out!

Circle the object that is different from the rest.

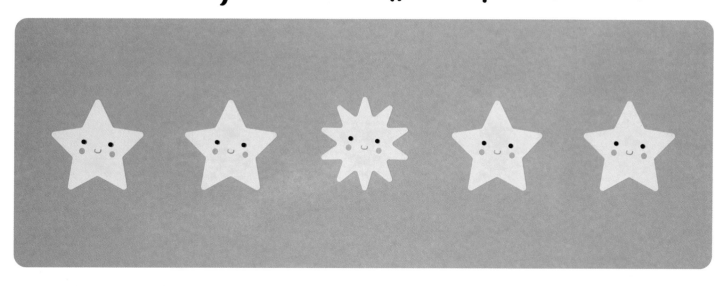

Fun with Shadows

Match these objects with their shadows.

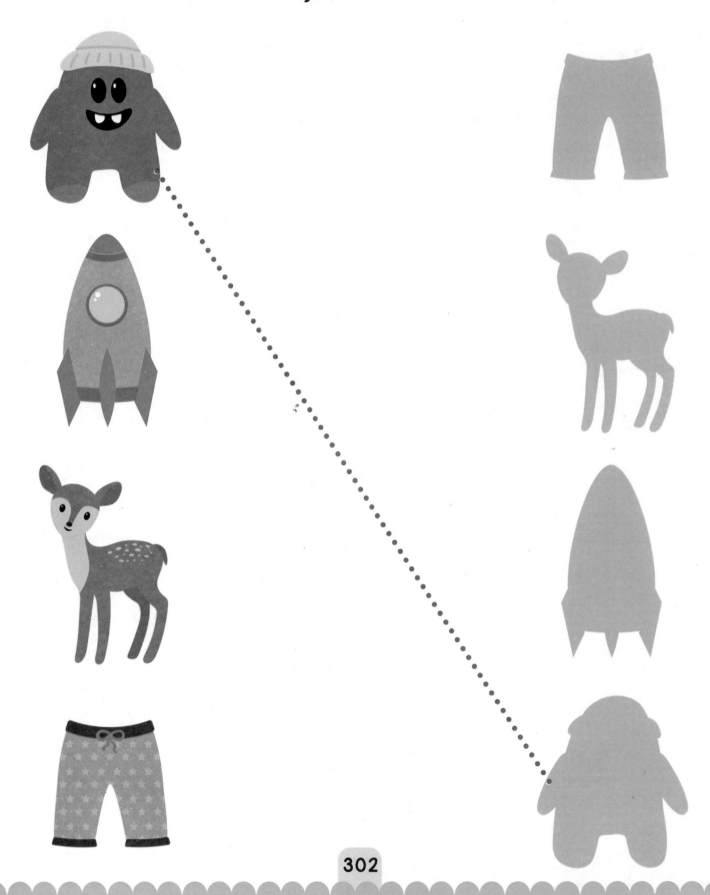

Fun with Shadows

Match these objects with their shadows.

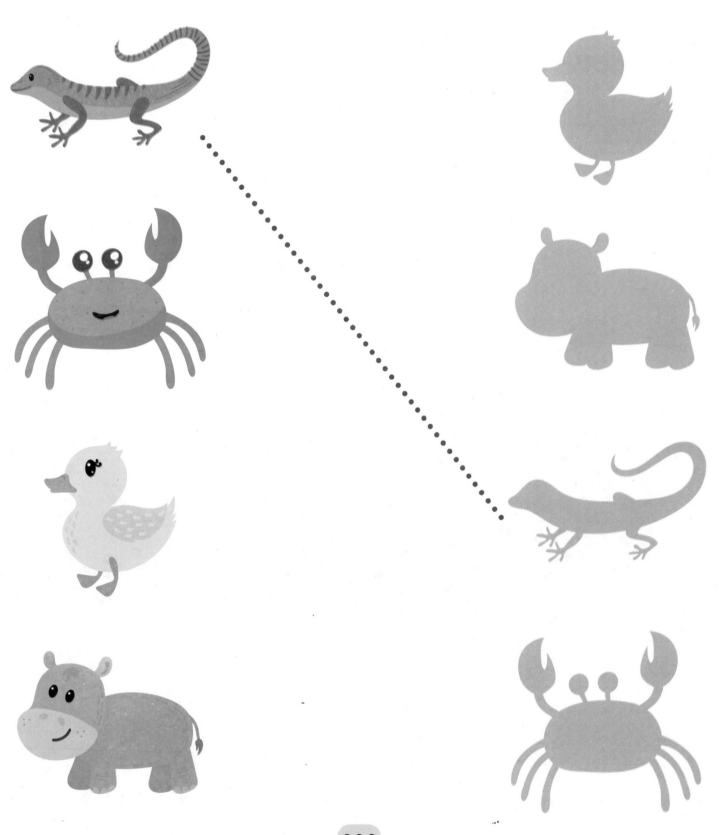

Find the Differences
Find and circle 7 differences between these pictures.

Find the Differences
Find and circle 5 differences between these the pictures.

Help squirrel find its food by following the arrows.

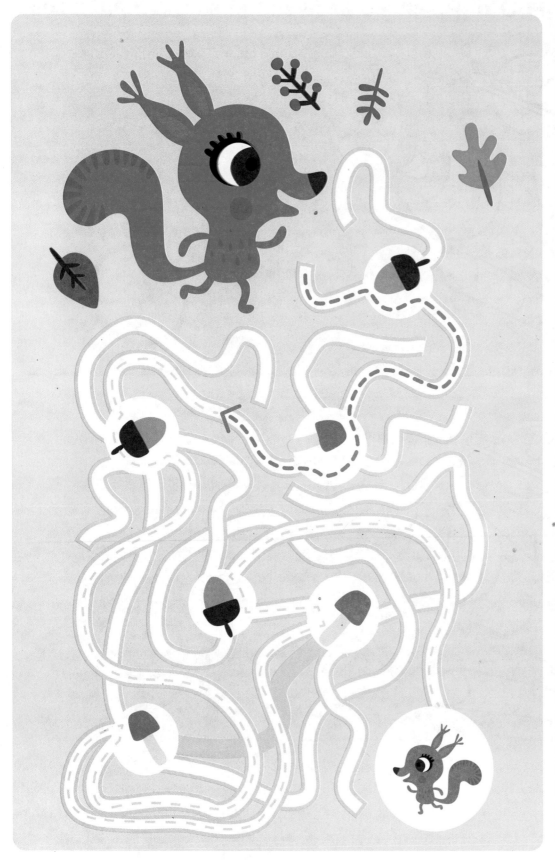

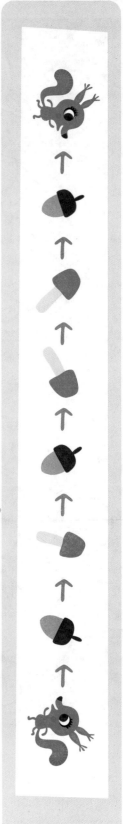

Help little dino find her mum!

little dino

mum

Color by Number

Color by Number

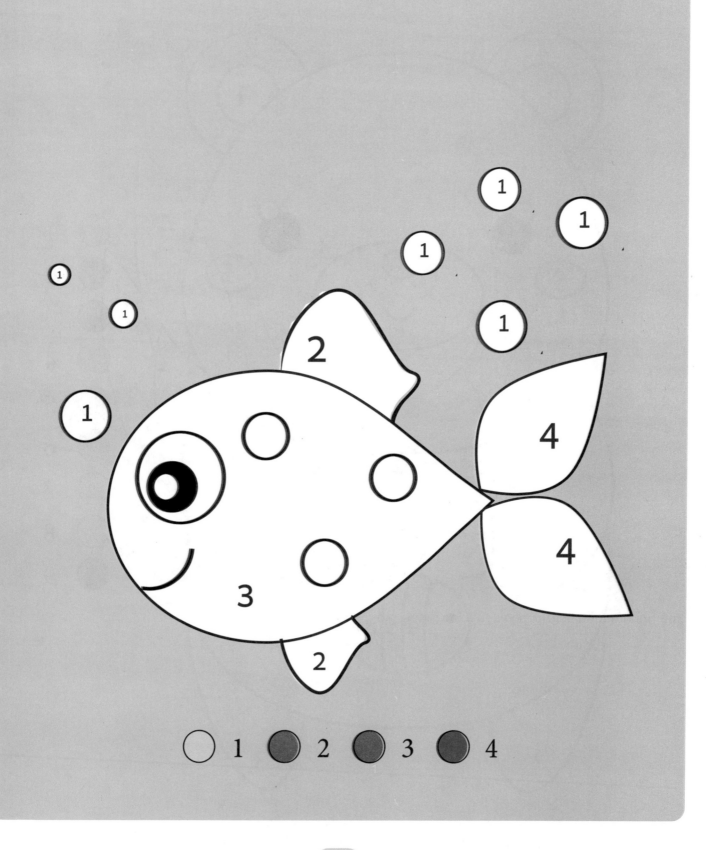

Color by Number

Color by Number

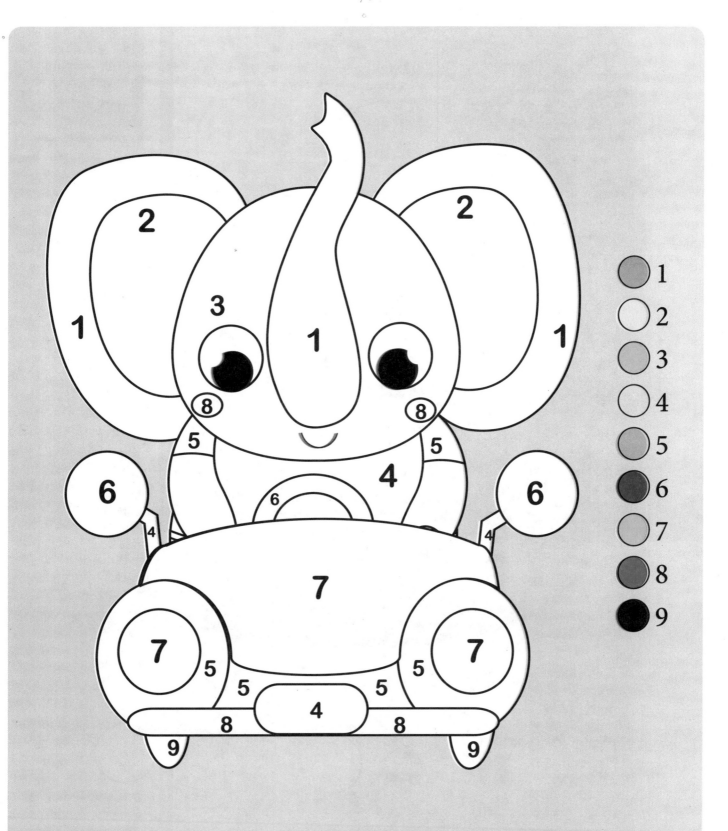

Count how many cake toppings are there and write the answers.

Count how many Christmas tree ornaments are there and write the answers.

Count and color the shapes on the fish.

Count, trace and color the shapes.

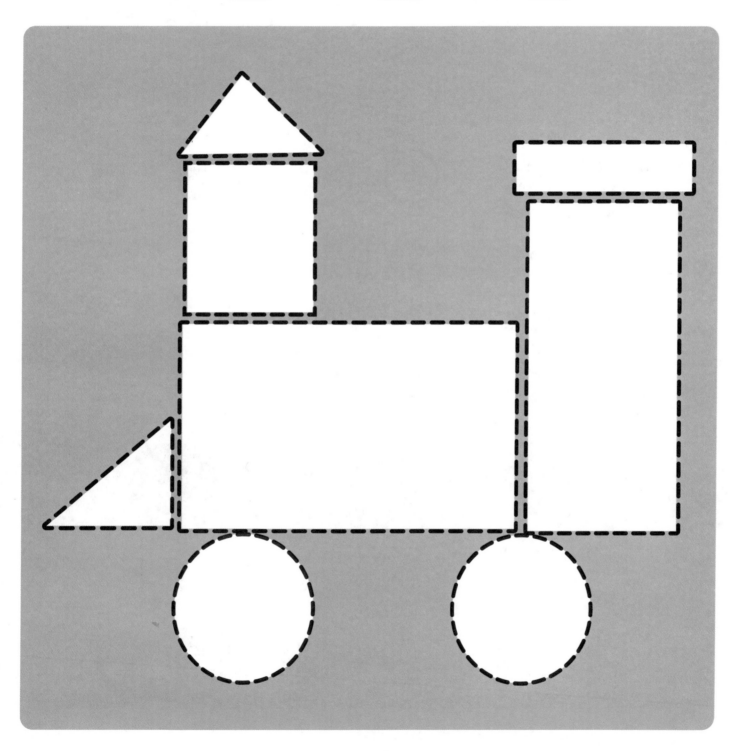

Circle the thing that does not belong!

Circle the thing that does not belong!

Count and write?

  [ ]   [ ]   [ ]   [ ]   [ ]

Finding Shapes

Count each shape given in the group below. Write the number next to its shape.

⬤ ·········   ▲ ·········   ▢ ·········   ◻ ·········

Match the number names.

5	ONE
8	TWO
1	THREE
6	FOUR
4	FIVE
2	SIX
3	SEVEN
10	EIGHT
9	NINE
7	TEN